About the Author

John Tully lives in Dover in the far south of Tasmania, but lived and worked in Melbourne for 35 years. He grew up in Tasmanian hydro construction towns after emigrating with his parents as a child from the UK. He is a semi-retired academic but 'in another life' he earned his living as a rigger in construction and heavy industry. He is the author of numerous non-fiction publications including a short history of Cambodia and a social history of the world rubber industry. John is a keen bushwalker. He has walked in many places around the world but believes that Tasmania is up there with the best of them. *On Shipstern Bluff* is his fifth novel and it continues the story of Hobart detective Jack Martin.

Also by John Tully

Novels

Death is the Cool Night

Robbed of Every Blessing

On an Alien Shore

Dark Clouds on the Mountain

Non-fiction Books Include

The Devil's Milk: A Social History of Rubber

A Short History of Cambodia

ON
SHIPSTERN
BLUFF

John Tully

This is a work of fiction. Except for historical figures and events, the characters, names, events and organisations in this story are fictional or are used fictitiously, and any resemblance to actual persons, businesses or organisations is entirely coincidental.

Published in 2021
©John Tully 2021

ISBN 9780645204506

Printed by Lightning Source
Melbourne, Australia
Set in 12/17 pt Minion Pro

ASHWOOD
PUBLISHING
Cradoc, Tasmania
info@ashwoodpublishing.com.au
https://ashwoodpublishing.com.au

A catalogue record for this work is available from the National Library of Australia

Cover design: Ashwood Publishing
Cover photo: Joel Everard/Shutterstock

In memory of Louis Bardenhagen, my inspirational English teacher at Launceston Matriculation College many decades ago.

Acknowledgements

I must thank my family for their love and support. Thanks also to Susan Young, whose close reading and thoughtful suggestions made this a better book.

The author and publisher wish to acknowledge and pay our respects to the Lyluequonny and Melukerdee people, the traditional owners and continuing custodians of Tasmania's Far South and the Huon Valley, the land on which this work was produced.

CHAPTER 1

THE SHEER DROP WAS TERRIFYING: five hundred feet of rushing air to the ocean far below. Jack imagined himself as Icarus, soaring high above Storm Bay, but not so high as to melt his wings in the fierce heat of the sun nor so low as to coat them in heavy salt spray and drop him into the ocean. He was perched on Shipstern Bluff, a tumble of cliffs rising dizzily from the surf heaving far below. Raucous seagulls wheeled and shrieked in the vast blue dome of the sky. Across the bay Mount Wellington humped on the skyline, shimmering in the haze. The heat was immense, the racket of the cicadas almost deafening. Far below, a pretty sailing ship tacked away from the rocky coast and faded into the cerulean expanse of the sea. It was one of those serene Tasmanian days when the sun seems to shine on a perfect world, but Jack was reminded of the Pieter Bruegel painting of the boy Icarus falling into the sea, while the ploughman ploughed on and a ship sailed off to wherever it had to go. Jack always had the ability—if that is the word—to stand outside of himself, and now he could see a trio of tiny figures kneeling on the bright green turf. An older man with greying hair was peering intently at what appeared to be a tailor's mannequin.

A quick headshake and Jack was back on solid ground, handkerchief pressed to his nose. The Vicks VapoRub almost masked the stink. There was nothing he could do about the flies. His companions, a young redheaded plainclothesman and an even younger uniformed police constable, were looking anywhere but at the corpse. The uniform, whose badge identified him as Junior Constable Kevin Gaffney, suddenly lurched to his feet and staggered to a clump of bushes and was violently and copiously sick.

Gaffney had met the detectives at the stile at Stormlea, where the gravel road ends and the walking track to Cape Raoul and Shipstern Bluff begins. A well-scrubbed young man with sticking-out ears, he was much in awe of the Hobart detectives; a Detective Inspector like Jack Martin was up there next to God. Jack had to ask him to slow down when he related what had happened, for the boy kept tripping over his tongue. Jack's offsider, Sergeant Bluey Bishop, rocked impatiently and ran his fingers through the red hair thick on his skull. 'Offer him a smoke,' Jack suggested, hoping it would calm Gaffney down.

The young man puffed gratefully and managed to marshal his thoughts. A 'photographer sheila' had found the body, he said, flicking through his notebook with a finger wetted with spit.

'Her name?' Bluey rolled his bloodshot eyes.

'Oh yairs! Annabelle van der M-Muh-Merwe,' Gaffney stammered.

Jack knew her: a petite but fit and strong young woman, she was an old friend of his daughter. She would most definitely give Constable Gaffney an earful if she heard him call her a sheila. She had managed to get a signal on her Nokia mobile phone and by the time she was nearing Stormlea, the two young police officers had come loping along like excited greyhounds and she'd walked back reluctantly to show them the body. Afterwards, she had followed one of them in her old bomb of a car to the police station at Dunalley. She was pretty shaken up but made a statement and agreed to call in at the Hobart police station the next day.

Jack and Bluey had arrived at Stormlea an hour or so later. Bluey had driven like a lunatic, not hesitating to use his blue flashing lamp and siren to shift the hat drivers and tractor wallahs clogging up the road. Jack had arranged for a helicopter to attend the scene but didn't fancy flying in it. The crew swore it had his fingerprints deep in the fuselage after the last time. Then again, whether flying was worse than Bluey Bishop's driving was a moot point. Bluey was well into his thirties, but in many ways, he was still the boy racer he had been when he came down from Burnie. Jack valued him as a good copper but at times he still felt like throttling him. He sprouted zits the size of Vesuvius and would still creep into work after a night on the tiles with love bites on his neck. Jack was also offended by his horrible ginger moustache, which looked like moths had been feeding on it.

Cigarettes and briefing finished, the party climbed over the stile and trudged through the late afternoon heat towards what Constable Gaffney referred to as 'the crime scene'. He fairly loped along on long Tasmanian footballer's legs with Bluey panting behind him. Jack's health regime must be working: he could keep up with the young fellow better than Bluey, who was soon wheezing like a ruptured Cajun squeezebox. The heat was stifling, and a mob of black cockatoos kept screeching, competing with the astounding din of the cicadas. A few times Bluey had to sit down and wipe the sweat off his face, but he made it to the top of the ridge and down to where the cliffs fell into the sea.

Jack was a reformed man. Some years back, a cheeky writer bloke had described him as 'a typical copper … stressed out most of the time, running on adrenaline, nicotine and coffee … running to flab from a diet of meat pies and sauce, chips and the deep-fried dog's turds they called chicken rolls.' Then he'd caught sight of his belly reflected in a shop window, wobbling like a blancmange. He'd binned the Camels and started going to the gym. Cut back on the booze and bought himself a pushbike and whizzed around the hilly streets of Sandy Bay and South Hobart. His daughter Wendy had been supportive and that helped. A lot of damage had been done, though. His nose was still knobbly: the grog does that to you, gives you a schnozz like W.C. Fields. Rhinophyma, his GP called it, but huffing and puffing on treadmills, Stairmasters, cross trainers, and other instruments of torture had melted away a lot of Jack's flab.

Bluey never let on how much dead bodies disturbed him, but he couldn't hide much from Jack, who had a good look for both of them. The inspection over, he stood up with a creak of his knees, brushing bits of grass from his trousers. He folded up his silver-framed glasses, which he was too vain to wear most of the time, put them in his breast pocket and wiped his hands on his handkerchief. He sighed. If only he could wipe away what he had just seen—this corpse of a child. It was a horrible sight that nobody except pathologists should ever see. The right leg was bent at an impossible angle. The back of the head had caved in and the brains had spattered out. The face was covered in bruises and lacerations. The poor hands were bloodied claws, and the eyes stared, open, bloodshot, and unseeing. Jack motioned his colleagues away from the body towards fresher air. He cocked his head, inviting Bluey to share his thoughts.

Bluey shrugged, sweating heavily. He'd complained of getting blisters from the hike in his city shoes. 'Looks like he fell from a great height, sir, but it's only a couple of feet from the clifftop to the ledge. Not enough to cause injuries like this.'

'Exactly what I'm thinking,' Jack replied. 'The slope of the land is hardly steep enough for the victim to have fallen so badly as to make such a mess of himself.'

'Yes, boss,' Bishop agreed. 'Now had he fallen down there'—he indicated the edge of the cliff with the toe of his crocodile skin shoe—'you could expect them kind of injuries.'

'Anyway,' Jack shrugged. 'We'll see what Dr Calvert says when he arrives.'

As if on cue, the helicopter's blades clattered overhead. The pilot circled round before spotting the men on the edge of the cliff. He would not find anywhere to land, just as Jack had figured when he decided to drive down from Hobart. Behind the cliffs, there were thickly wooded hills and although it might at a pinch be possible to land further towards Cape Raoul, there was no guarantee of it, given the density of the coastal scrub. Whoever wished to land here would have to be winched down and the helicopter team were well prepared for this. Two human figures, strapped face to face, descended on an impossibly thin cable that spooled out of the belly of the helicopter whirring above. Jack felt sick with vertigo just looking at them, full of an irrational fear that the cable might snap and drop them to their deaths. One of the figures was clutching a battered old Gladstone bag, once common in Australia but now carried only by a dwindling band of old men. The owner's sunset years, however, were far off. The pair landed safely on the turf and disentangled themselves from the safety harness with its bewildering profusion of clips and belts.

'Dr Calvert, I presume,' Jack intoned with a mock bow to the smaller of the two daredevils, a slight figure with a starburst of auburn hair and a wispy orange beard.

'Ah, the famous Detective Inspector Jack Martin himself,' Calvert chuckled, already snapping open the clasps of his Gladstone bag, 'and his trusty sidekick Detective Sergeant Bluey Bishop I do declare.'

Calvert dropped the bag to the ground and fished a packet of 'Drum' tobacco and papers from his New Zealand bush shirt. Jack watched him closely, still hungry for a smoke despite giving up some years before. Once, he recalled, Dr Simon Calvert, assistant pathologist to Professor Peregrine Rowley-Samuels, used to smoke the lethal 'White Ox' tobacco. 'Drum' was his concession to the health warnings his profession dished out to the rest of humanity—including Jack, who had once had a hacking smoker's cough from unfiltered Camels.

'Mind you don't contaminate the crime scene, Simon,' Jack warned. 'Duncan Snodgers and his team will make my life a misery if you do.'

He should have saved his breath. Calvert and his boss, the professor, were a law unto themselves, an elite whose occupation was beyond the ken of most people and bestowed certain privileges upon them. Calvert waved a hand airily, dismissing Jack's mild remonstration.

'Now, what have you got for me, Jack? Looks a bit grim, eh?' If the pathologist was disconcerted by the horrible sight and smell, it didn't show on his boyish features.

'Grim's about right,' Jack grunted. 'Young fella. Just a kid. Foreign looking, maybe. He's been pretty badly knocked around but in my opinion he—'

'Well, Inspector, we'll save your layman's opinion if you don't mind.' Calvert was getting to be as blunt as his boss. 'I'll tell you *what* happened and then you can tell me later *why* it happened, *who dunnit* and all that.' He waved a dismissive hand and knelt next to the corpse to begin his examination.

Jack gave him the finger but made sure his subordinates didn't see.

Above them, the helicopter climbed into the sky, clattering eastward over the hills towards Port Arthur. The crewman had been winched back up but had promised to return to pick up the pathologist and lower some of the equipment of the Scene-of-Crime Officers who were reportedly walking from Stormlea.

'Hmmm … Quite dead … Multiple fractures in the legs and arms … probably elsewhere too, but we'll know for sure when we get him on the slab … Extensive bruising … Lacerations … Back of the head has an open wound … I'd say he clearly fell or was pushed from a considerable height. But even the rookie constable over there'—he indicated Gaffney with his chin—'would know that.'

'Yeah, we know he's dead, mate,' Jack grumped.

'Yes, yes, patience Jack,' Calvert advised. 'Already there are signs of decomposition …'

'And how long …' essayed Bishop boldly, given that he normally treated the pathologist as a wizard involved in esoteric horror.

Calvert ignored him and fished round inside his bag until he found a thermometer. 'Roll him over, would you?' he muttered. Bluey complied and looked away as the pathologist took a rectal temperature reading. 'No sign of rigor mortis, so that narrows it down a bit. Now, if you'll excuse me, I'll get on with my preliminary examination. What I can tell you is that his injuries are consistent with a fall from a great height.'

'So it would have been the fall that killed him?'

'Certainly looks like it, Jack. No evidence of any other explanation unless the autopsy reveals it.'

Jack jerked his head to one side, signalling to Bluey and Gaffney that they should leave the pathologist mumbling to himself about Glaister equations and rectal temperatures. He'd tell them in his own good time.

'Let's have a look around before Mr Snodgers gets here,' Jack suggested and it didn't take them long to find smears of blood and what looked like dried porridge on the rocks, though even Gaffney guessed it was brains.

After just a little while, Calvert called them back over. 'Now Jack,' he said. 'I can't give you a definitive answer at this stage, but I'd say he died three days ago. It's been very hot as you know and as you can see with the heat the flies have got to him and incubated their eggs. Maggots would've been incubated quite recently ...'

Constable Gaffney ran off again dry-retching violently, and Calvert raised his eyebrows in mock surprise. 'What did I say?' he smirked. 'It seems I'm always upsetting someone.' He was getting to be as bad as his boss, the professor. Scenes such as this still horrified Jack and he'd seen a depressing number of corpses after other humans had finished with them.

Just then, there was the sound of many voices from up the hillside. The Scene-Of-Crime team had arrived, headed by a profusely sweating Duncan Snodgers and guided by a young female copper, Constable Pru Skinner. Jack felt sorry for the SOCOs, forced to carry heavy equipment along the steep track in the immense heat. The photographer, Dave Oaten, was making particularly heavy weather of it. Jack had to admit to some malicious joy at the sight of their sweaty boss, who had discarded his suit jacket.

'Must be a first,' whispered Jack, with a wink to Calvert. 'Bugger only takes it off when he puts on the kilt and sporran for Burns Nights.'

'Och, Jack,' Snodgers grumbled. 'Ye couldnae make it a wee bit more difficult to get to?'

A ponderous man who had thickened over the years to almost the same width as his height, he was mopping a brow that was already showing signs of painful sunburn. Jack felt guilty for his Schadenfreude, and he liked the bloke too.

'They bloody cockatoos wouldnae stop shrieking and there were snakes—yes, bloody *snakes*—sunning themselves on the path. Bodies falling oot o' the sky like they was Icarus. And you, Dr Calvert,' he added, scowling at the pathologist, 'ye've bin smoking at a crime scene again!'

Jack laughed. 'Well, it's all yours now, Duncan. We're off. We'll have a beer for you in the Dunalley pub.'

'O aye,' said the Scot ruefully. 'Think o' me when ye're boozing in whatever dive you end up in.' Sighing audibly, he summoned his team together for instructions before they began what Jack knew would be an exacting search of the crime scene.

The helicopter had returned. The cable snaked from its belly and whisked Calvert swiftly upwards after he had tried in vain to coax Jack to accompany him. Jack had never had a head for heights and not even the thought of the long slog back to Stormlea through the overheated bush could make him change his mind. Gaffney and Pru Skinner had already scooted off up the track, as sure-footed as goats, seemingly unaffected by the heat and eager to get away from the body. Duncan Snodgers and his long-suffering team would collect all the forensic evidence they could. A large tent, generator and lighting equipment would soon be winched down from the helicopter and the team would work away into the night. Possibly all night. They'd snack on stale sandwiches and lukewarm tea, and piss in the bushes at a safe distance. The cadaver itself would be zipped into a thick black plastic body bag and winched upward. Kevin Gaffney and Pru Skinner would never see it again, but Jack knew that he and Bluey would re-acquaint themselves with it the next morning in Simon Calvert's domain, the Hobart mortuary. He was expecting them at 9:00 am sharp.

CHAPTER 2

JACK HAD ALWAYS HATED the sight of the bodies the pathologists filleted and sewed back up. He had never got used to the whine of the circular saw, the rummaging about in body cavities and skulls, and the sloppy thump of organs landing on the scales. He was still as revolted by the smells and gurgling noises as he'd been the first time he was in the mortuary. Autopsies were powerful reminders of his own mortality, but he also felt an aching sadness for the people struck down before their time, and for their grieving relatives. This case was worse because the victim was just a kid. Jack knew that the body on the slab was no longer a person, knew that the spark of life was gone, that only a husk was left, but the knowledge didn't make the proceedings any easier to take. He wondered if religious belief would make it easier, but his Catholicism had lapsed years before.

Simon Calvert took his time, methodically examining the corpse, with his red hair spilling out at the sides of his surgical cap. His assistant, a heavy-set young woman similarly masked and garbed, stood attentively close by, ready to jump to his commands. He began to examine every inch of the corpse's exterior, muttering inaudibly except when he ordered the assistant to turn the body this way or that, sometimes mumbling to himself and at other times speaking clearly and calmly into the microphone.

'As you are aware, the body has been in the hot sun and putrefaction is advanced,' he noted. 'It's been mauled by animals. Maybe Tassie Devils, but I can't be definitive.'

Jack gave silent thanks for the powerful exhaust fans. He had also long ago perfected the art of allowing his eyes to glaze over so that he was spared the worst sights.

'I'd put the age of this young male at between 13 and 14 years,' said Calvert. 'He's of Balkan appearance, perhaps, which may be relevant, Jack. Small for his years, too.' He muttered something inaudible as he inserted a periodontal probe into the mouth. 'Hmm … poor dentition … advanced caries in the upper and lower jaw … signs of periodontal disease, indicating long periods of neglect. Unusual to be so advanced in one so young.'

Jack averted his eyes when the assistant turned the body on its front and Calvert continued his examination.

After some minutes and some more probing, Calvert spoke directly to the detectives. 'There's something else, Jack,' he sighed, 'but I'll come back to this later.'

The autopsy reached the stage that Jack dreaded. The assistant stepped forward and deftly wielded a scalpel to make a Y-shaped incision in the front of the torso. The business of rummaging, slicing, gouging, and weighing began. Yet, Simon Calvert was as respectful as it was possible to be when doing such things to a human body.

'Last meal, probably baked beans on toast, well-digested now.'

Bluey Bishop shifted from foot to foot and looked like he would enjoy a cigarette. The dismal business went on, with a pair of shears being used to crack through the ribs so that what lay beneath could be examined.

Finally, Calvert turned and spread out his hands, which were clad in bloodstained rubber gloves. 'The body has massive injuries, Jack, and any one of them could have killed him. There are multiple compound fractures, lacerations, and bruising, along with massive internal injuries to all the organs. It's as if the unfortunate young man has been in a high-speed collision or fallen from a great height.' He patted his chest nervously before remembering that his tobacco was elsewhere. 'I hate to tell you this, Jack,' he said, almost in a whisper, 'but someone has sexually interfered with the poor kid.'

Jack closed his eyes, fighting back the urge to shout and swear. He knew that he had to stand back and take the information dispassionately, but he never could. Simon Calvert nodded sadly before turning back to the dissection table. Jack was relieved when the assistant began to sew up the body with thick black twine and the detectives were free to go. They were walking out of the mortuary when Professor Rowley-Samuels hove into view, immaculately dressed as usual in a brown suit and bow tie.

'How did my communist boy go?' he demanded, with the snorting laugh that was his trademark. 'Solved the case for you, has he?'

Rowley-Samuels always referred to his understudy in this way because Calvert's left-wing views were a source of mingled puzzlement, disapproval, and mirth for him. Now nudging thirty, Calvert would always be a boy to the ageing pathologist.

'Well Prof,' Jack replied, 'as you would expect, your boy was thorough. He ascertained the cause of death and supplied some other details, but it's up to us plods to discover the *hows, whys* and *whos* of the child's death. We're waiting on his full report.'

'Child?' queried the Prof, his face suddenly puckered with concern, no longer snorting with laughter. 'You said 'child'?' Jack confirmed this was the case and the professor went back into his office shaking his head.

After a quick cup of coffee in the Carlton café, Jack and Bluey crossed the street to the police station. A group of young nurses passed them at the crossing, chattering brightly, and cars honked impatiently at the traffic lights. Life was going on as normal in Hobart Town, and Jack thought again of the Icarus painting. There was a poem too, he recalled, by W.H. Auden. An ekphrastic poem, that was the word. A poem describing a work of art. It was in a volume of verse on his daughter's English Literature reading list.

Annabelle van der Merwe was already waiting in the interview room. She declined the offer of tea or coffee, explaining that she had an employment interview she couldn't afford to miss. Jack liked her, although as a veteran of the forest blockades she was precisely the kind of young woman calculated to enrage some of his colleagues. Whippet-thin and fit, she was nevertheless very pretty; blond-haired and blue eyed, the epitome of a Dutch girl from a flat landscape dotted with windmills. In fact, she came from South Africa, and she had a strong Boer-inflected accent. Jack recalled her as an intense schoolgirl, waving anti-apartheid placards in the Elizabeth Street Mall a few years back, much to her Calvinist parents' disapproval. While Bluey fiddled around with the recording apparatus, she asked Jack how his daughter, Wendy, was going on her overseas trip. He knew they were good friends. Bluey signalled that they were ready, and they got down to business.

Annabelle explained that she had been walking along the track to Cape Raoul two days earlier when she got a whiff of something dead. She had been curious but didn't investigate because she wanted to get to the Cape to take photographs of the seals before the sun went down. She was on her first paid assignment for a geographical magazine and was anxious to make a good job of it. Besides, animals died, she shrugged, and with weather like this it wasn't surprising something would stink. The weather might have broken, and she might have missed the best light for photographs. A keen rock climber, she had abseiled down the dolerite cliffs to get as close as possible to the seal haul-out. The pictures would be brilliant, she said.

She had camped out on the Cape for the night and unpitched her tent the next morning after a leisurely breakfast of muesli, and coffee brewed on her spirit stove. She was in no hurry to get back and was enjoying the unusual warmth of the sun. She decided to use up the rest of her film with some photos of the fluted dolerite columns and some long-distance shots of Cape Pillar, so it was late morning before she shouldered her pack and started back along the track to Stormlea. Toiling up the hill off the flat lozenge of the peninsula, she caught the stench again and a glimpse of something bright orange coloured impelled her to investigate. Dropping her rucksack, she made her way down the side track to Shipstern Bluff and looked down to where the land sloped away to the edge of the abyss. She wished she hadn't, for there, lying on its back was a human body and from its utter stillness she knew this was no peripatetic sunbather or tired surfer. It appeared to be a young male, but she didn't go close enough to be sure.

Jack thanked Annabelle. He would arrange for someone to bring a typed version of her statement for her to sign. He escorted her to the front door and promised to tell Wendy that he had met her.

Two days later, after reading Calvert's final report and Duncan Snodgers' conclusions from the crime scene, Jack briefed the squad of detectives whom Derek Holmes had assigned to the case. There were no fingerprints and nothing to suggest that anyone except the police, the pathologist and Ms van der Merwe had recently been in the vicinity. Nor were there any clues to the victim's identity. There was evidence of sexual interference and there were traces of flunitrazepam— also known as rohypnol—in the bloodstream. Someone must have taken the boy to Shipstern Bluff and dropped him onto the clifftop from a great height from an aircraft. Maybe the idea had been for him to fall all the way down to the wave-cut platform at the foot of the cliffs to make it look like an accident—rock climbers often scaled the cliffs in the vicinity.

Rookie Constable Kate Farrar put her hand up, intent but nervous. 'Any possibility he was dead before the fall, sir?'

'The pathologist couldn't rule it out for certain, but all the evidence suggests he was killed by the fall,' replied Jack, impressed by the young woman's nous. 'And we have to ask why would anyone go to the trouble of flying a body out to Shipstern Bluff when they could have buried it? Any amount of remote bush in Tasmania.'

It still begged the question of why the boy's life had ended on the frayed edge of the Tasman Peninsula. Jack turned and wrote the words 'WHY SHIPSTERN?' In block capitals on the whiteboard and circled them in red. The room had fallen silent as the officers imagined the boy's last, terrifying moments.

'OK,' said Jack. 'Let's get out and catch whoever did this.'

The officers shuffled out quietly, only breaking into sub-dued chatter when they had left the briefing room. Bluey and another constable left to check the light aviation firms for any suspicious activity. Later that afternoon, Jack made a televised appeal for anyone who had any information that might help the police inquiry to come forward. Somebody had mentioned to the press that Jack had dubbed the victim 'Icarus' and for better or worse, it stuck.

CHAPTER 3

JACK WOKE UP FEELING SEEDY and disgusted with himself. Yesterday's lunch, wolfed down in the car between the cop shop and a break-and-enter scene in North Hobart, had consisted of an industrial meat pie and a so-called quiche that had oozed some disgusting white substance all over his shirtfront. Tea, as many Tasmanians still called the evening meal, was three packets of salt and vinegar chips washed down with numerous beers at the Royal Exchange pub in the company of his old mates Sergeants Fuller and Langdale, both still attempting Beatle haircuts despite their receding hairlines and expanding waists. As Jack had feared, the Shipstern murder case had got to him. 'Bottle it up and it comes out to bite you,' Dr Ziegler had warned. 'And you'll be back on the grog.' He bolted a slice of toast and jam—bugger the yoghurt and muesli today—and drank two cups of tea liberally doused with sugar. It would have to stop before he slid back into the lifestyle he had promised Wendy he'd quit for good. After gobbling some paracetamol and scrubbing away his sins in a long hot shower, he felt almost human. He fed Wendy's silver tabby cat Norman—no idea why she had to call a female cat Norman—and set off for work.

The televised appeal yielded nothing except crazed telephone calls from an assortment of nutters who were 'known to the police'. Nor did other inquiries turn up anything of value. The mad old bat Mabel Triffitt claimed aliens had done it—the same perverts who had been nicking her smalls off the Hills Hoist. Alderman Audrey Amos speculated that communists had done it, and celebrity journalist Chuck Laineux lambasted 'police incompetence'. The light aviation companies had been busy, but none of their aircraft had been near the Tasman Peninsula and an examination of their logbooks backed them up. Nor did Jack's snouts know anything of value. The case had stalled, and he went home that night despairing, but virtuously abstemious.

The late summer heatwave had ended, and Hobart's variable weather was back. He had kept the house in Darcy Street when Helen left him for the man he thought of as 'that teacher bloke'. Wendy had gone off backpacking in South America with her entitled rich kid boyfriend, a wanker who blathered incessantly about how everything was so much bigger and better back 'Stateside'. The house was too big for Jack, but he had stayed out of inertia and the vain hope that Helen would return. Fat chance of that now—she had filed for divorce and he worried about having to sell the house to pay for her half share. Dismissing these thoughts, he parked his car in the street, intending to drive later to the supermarket. After drinking a cup of tea with some more paracetamol to tackle the remains of the hangover, he decided that the supermarket could wait, so the car stayed outside in the street. He went to bed early after switching off the television in disgust: had thrown his slippers at it when the Prime Minister came on sounding more constipated than usual with that whiny, hard-done-by expression and Cheshire cat grin. Snodgers called Howard an 'auld cockwomble' and it fit.

The following day, Jack's hangover had abated, and he trotted down the front path in good humour, jiggling his car keys. The mood evaporated when he saw his car slumped on the road like a sad old basset hound: some bastard had slashed all four of his tyres! Duncan Snodgers arrived promptly but could find no clues to the vandal's identity and the neighbours had seen nothing, not even old Mrs Hitzenbichler who usually saw everything and didn't seem to sleep. The neighbours' cars were unscathed, so it seemed that whoever had done it had it in for Jack. Next, while he was at work, someone burgled the house. They had disarmed the alarm system, suggesting a greater degree of sophistication than that possessed by the average Taswegian burglar, and then thoroughly ransacked the place. A few valuable items were missing—including the Wedgwood tea set that Helen had inexplicably left behind—but it seemed that the purpose of the break-in was to create the maximum amount of damage. Norman had wisely fled the *locus in quo*, and Jack only coaxed her back inside with difficulty. His left eye was twitching ominously.

Mrs Hitzenbichler said '*Ja*, I have noticed a man in overalls going onto the property in the late *Morgen*, err morning.' She added that he had parked a white tradesman's van outside and as she believed he must have been a plumber or a painter, she had given him no more thought. Her description of the man was vague.

'He was wearing von of dem peaked cap dingies,' she told Sergeant Fuller.

'A baseball cap?'

'*Ja*, dat's der one.'

She told Fuller the man had dark hair but had second thoughts and informed Langdale that his hair was 'how do you say, mouse-like,' and she could not say if he was tall, short, thin or fat. 'My eyesight is not what it used to be,' she sighed. She had not recorded the van's numberplate. 'It was *sehr schmutzig*, very dirty,' she did recall. 'And it had a big dent in der backside.' She pondered a while as the detectives drank their coffee and munched a second helping of her home baked *Lebkuchen*. '*Ach*, I am a silly old woman. *Dachschaden, ich glaube! Vielleicht es war blau nicht schwarz!* Blue, you know!' Duncan Snodgers went through the house meticulously but found nothing. The intruder had been wearing gloves and apart from a couple of footprints, which turned out to be of generic Adidas-type soles, there was no forensic evidence.

Jack nodded his head when Sergeant Fuller reported all this to him. The crimes seemed personal. The chances were that the bastard wouldn't stop at burglary and slashing tyres and if so, they'd catch him. In the meantime, it was good that Wendy was overseas. He shuddered to think what might have happened if she'd been at home when the creep in white overalls came visiting.

***

Some months had passed since the Shipstern horror, and Jack was no closer to solving the mystery. The earth was turning on its axis and the lengthening shadows of autumn were falling across Jack's back lawn. It was time to clean out the leaves from the gutters and batten down for the approaching winter. Despite the chores, autumn was Jack's favourite season. To clear his mind after work, he took his bike out of the shed and rode down the impossibly steep Lynton Avenue. On a whim, he braved the late afternoon traffic on Sandy Bay Road, giving a hoon the finger on the way, and stopped for a breather in St David's Park. The European trees were a riot of yellows, oranges, reds and russets and the stone walls kept out the worst of the traffic noise. The flower beds gave off a rich plumcake smell, and the gardener was packing up his tools. He looked familiar, but Jack couldn't place him, and they exchanged friendly nods. The earth was preparing for its annual sleep. At times like this, Jack felt at peace with the world. Yet a shadow passed over him. This place had been the colonial graveyard, and Jack imagined the flogging parson Bobby Knopwood droning the last prayers over the grave of some poor wretch. T.S. Eliot was right, Jack thought as the trees stretched long fingers of shade towards him across the grass: fear stalks in our shadows. It was time to go.

It was dark when Jack got home and parked his trusty steed in the shed. Life seemed good. He was in the back kitchen heating up last night's chicken curry when the big picture window that looked out over the garden exploded into a thousand fragments. He instinctively threw himself to the floor with only a millisecond to spare before another burst of gunfire sprayed into the back wall of what he called the 'scout hall'—the large extension he and Helen had built. Then silence. Jack sat up against the wall and swore as he brushed shattered glass from his clothes. The fucking bastards had gone too far! When he had finished, he crawled on his hands and knees to the telephone and rang the police station. As he suspected, the shooter was long gone by the time the cavalry arrived with sirens blaring and lights flashing. They walked in the front door just as Jack was surveying the damage and promising vengeance on the culprits.

Fuller and Langdale calculated that the shooter had fired from a position forty yards away on the back fence line of Jack's garden. The owners of the adjacent property, from which the gunman had fired off a magazine, were overseas and none of the other neighbours had seen or heard anything. Snodgers did find an Adidas footprint identical to the ones left by the burglar who had slashed Jack's tyres. He believed that the weapon used was probably a Colt AR-15, a semi-automatic carbine like the military M16; the same type as the one used by the lunatic in the Port Arthur massacre and recently banned by the federal government. The bullets embedded in the wall were Remington .223 calibre and Snodgers guessed that the shooter had used a suppressor to dampen the noise. Jack wondered why the shooter had not hit him: was it because he was a bad shot or was he still just trying to scare him? He didn't argue when Derek Holmes, the new commander, ordered him to move into a police safe house in Moonah.

'Who has it in for you, Jack?' Holmes asked, slurping his tea and nibbling on a Scotch Finger biscuit. With the stripe of white in his black hair, he reminded Jack of a magpie or a Collingwood player. Had the beak too, and a pair of unblinking green eyes that did not miss much. Jack had stopped giving people nicknames, but he wondered about his boss.

'Well,' Jack shrugged, 'I've put away enough villains over the years and some of them must hate my guts, but the ones that spring to mind are all either dead or else are over the river in the Pink Palace.' Most crims, he knew, lived by a code that included never going after an officer or his family, although there were exceptions.

'What about the Nazis?' Holmes asked. 'Have any of them been released recently?'

Half a decade ago, Jack had arrested a whole Storm Troop of Hitler fans who had been peddling drugs and persecuting members of the small Jewish and Asian communities. Although their *Führer* Jamie Sheather and his deputy Michael Blander were serving life sentences for murder in Risdon Prison—nicknamed the Pink Palace because of the coloured concrete used in its construction—some of their underlings must have served their sentences.

'Then there's Angelo Mitropoulos,' mused Holmes, reaching for another biscuit. 'He's doing a very long stretch and if anyone hates your guts, it's him.'

Jack had an image of Mitropoulos in his mind's eye—a flash, boofy narcissist draped in gold jewellery. What was it Simon Calvert had called him—'a member of the illegal bourgeoisie'—a drugs tsar who had managed to continue running his businesses from prison. He was worth considering. He had been a business associate of the Nazis and was a murderer too, and it was Jack who had put him away. According to the police snouts, though, another firm was muscling in on the city's drug trade.

'Any connection with the Shipstern Bluff murder, do you think?' wondered Holmes as he refilled Jack's cup with a vastly superior brew to the swill in the canteen. 'You've taken a high profile on that case.'

Jack shrugged. 'We're no closer to solving that, I'm afraid, so I doubt that anyone feels I'm treading on their toes. Still, it's always possible.'

Holmes sighed. 'There's so many of them that they could be queueing up to have a pop at you! You'll have to move straight away, cat and all.' He smiled wanly. 'Now means now … Giacomo.' Holmes's predecessor, Booker Sahib as they called him, had told the bastard Jack was Giacomo Martinuzzi on his birth certificate. Holmes loved to tease him about it, although the truth was that after Jack learned about his dad, he had considered reverting to the name.

Wendy, for her part, always reacted furiously when anyone mocked their Italian heritage. 'Fucking racists give me the shits,' she would rant.

'Pottymouth.' Jack would never get used to the idea of his little girl swearing.

'Well they do, Dad!'

***

'Hey, Jack,' said Liz Flakemore, sliding into his spare office chair. 'Marg and me are going for a day walk in the Hartz Mountains next Sunday. You're welcome to come.'

'Wouldn't I be a gooseberry?'

'Nah, I wouldn't ask if you were. You need to get out of yourself. I'm worried all the stress'll make you backslide into your bad old ways.'

'Yes, mum,' he laughed.

Marg was Liz's new lover; a slight, dark-haired, rather taciturn young woman. Jack had to admit to the slightest twinge of jealousy, but he knew Liz 'played for the other side', and besides, she was too young for him. He sensed that Marg's reserve was directed at him. Soon they were driving south over Vince's Saddle into the verdant valley of the Huon River. It was a glorious day, and the countryside was bedecked in all its russet and gold autumn finery. The Huon comes as a surprise, its green hills and fertile paddocks protected from the Roaring Forties by a wall of mountains to the west. Jack was absorbed by the landscape but Liz was pensive as she steered round the tight bends through Longley and down towards Grove, with its miles of orchards.

'Penny for them, Liz,' said Marg; the first words she had spoken in a while.

'You can relax,' Liz replied. 'I should have told you. Jack is one of the good guys. He was a huge support to me when I came out at work. He was as horrified by the way the police acted in the gay rights protests as I was.'

When Liz was still a constable, Jack had persuaded her not to resign after the arrest of demonstrators calling for the repeal of Tasmania's draconian anti-homosexual laws.

'You can get 21 bloody years!' Liz had raged, her green eyes flashing. 'Tasmania still has the world's highest rates of incarceration for sex between consenting adult males!'

Indeed, in a piece of reactionary theatre orchestrated by local and state politicians, the officers had donned rubber gloves to ward off AIDS when they swarmed down to Salamanca Place to arrest the protesters. 'Homosexuals are not welcome in Tasmania,' growled the 'whispering bulldozer', state premier Robin Gray. Not to be outdone, a zealot in the Legislative Council had urged that 'poofters' should be 'tracked down and wiped out by the police.'

His words were chilling.

'Did you know,' Liz had told Jack, 'that in 1867, Tasmania was the last place in the British Empire to put a man to death for consensual sodomy?'

She had kept quiet about her sexuality until the Salamanca

arrests, but after that she didn't deny that she was a lesbian, and Jack had stuck by her against the sniggers and sneers of Eric Blundstone and his medieval colleagues.

Marg didn't say anything, but Jack could tell that she was relieved. She insisted on buying when they stopped for coffee in Huonville, and by the time they turned off the highway at Geeveston to begin the climb to the mountains she was chatting happily with Jack about her work as a music teacher and her ambition for further study in Vienna.

Jack exulted to be alive when they picked their way along the walking track under the Devils Backbone to begin the steep ascent past Lake Esperance to the summit of Hartz Peak. He didn't wheeze and could keep up with his companions, and felt virtuous for giving up the Camels and the constant irrigation of his liver. They sat on the rocks at the summit to eat their sandwiches, grateful for the warmth of the low sun on their backs. The view was stupendous, but a shadow crossed Jack's mind when he saw, far away across the ragged coastline of Bruny Island, Shipstern Bluff and Cape Raoul rising from the heaving sea. Just then, a faint drone broke the silence. It was a tiny aeroplane flashing silver in the sun. It had come from the north and was circling down towards where the town of Huonville lay in the folds of the valley.

'Strange,' Liz murmured. 'I wouldn't have thought there was an airstrip anywhere down there.'

Jack shrugged, but he looked thoughtful as he began to stuff things back into his rucksack for the walk back down the mountain.

CHAPTER 4

THE POLICE SAFE HOUSE IN MOONAH was a dismal place wedged into a south-facing hillside. Functional and cold, smelling of stale takeaways and damp, it seemed to know it was unloved and had given up trying. Squatting between a soulless box of brick flats and a bakery, its mean little windows had turned their backs on a fine view over the river. Jack hated it and after a week, it was beginning to give him cabin fever. Norman loathed the place too and showed her displeasure by shitting on the lime-green and orange carpet. Jack wondered if it had been built by old Roman Ferenczak, the tyrannical father of his former girlfriend, for he had lived nearby and rented out similar architectural warts. Whoever wrote that M.A.S.H song about suicide being painless might have lived in such a hopeless place. And if they'd stocked the kitchenette, they must have lived on microwaved meals as it lacked the utensils that made for a civilised existence. The stove should have been shot at dawn. It took forever to heat up and then would burn your dinner when your back was turned. Jack reached into the bar fridge for yet another microwave ham and pineapple pizza but put it back and slammed the door. Bugger it. He would put his coat on and wander down to the Golden Dragon, the Chinese restaurant on the main road. Again.

Even with his warm coat on, it was frigid outside, with a bone-chilling wind whistling off the mountain and a frost beginning to sparkle on the road. It was lonely too, to see happy families snug in front of the TV sets that winked in green unison all along the street. Jack felt a sudden craving for company and wondered if he should get another dog. His old bitzer Rosie had died and he didn't have the heart to get a replacement, but maybe it was time, though he fretted that dogs didn't live long enough. Maybe he'd get a golden retriever. Everyone praised them as beautiful, intelligent and affectionate, but warned they shed fur and clogged up vacuum cleaners.

Walking down a gloomy cul-de-sac to a pedestrian walk-way, he found himself thinking of Helen. They hadn't had a bad marriage. They'd had their ups and downs, but then that bloody teacher bloke had come along. Lance Weaver or Beaver or whatever the fucker's name was. Helen had enrolled in an Adult Ed. English Literature course and had gone up to some poncy place called The Grange in Campbell Town for a weekend retreat. The tutor was the Weaver-Beaver bloke. Afterwards it was 'Mr Weaver this' and 'Mr Beaver that' and after another session, it was Lance this, that and the other. The woman was smitten. One evening when he'd fed Norman and was getting ready for bed, she had blurted out that she had met someone and was leaving. He should have seen it coming, but then he would be the last person to know, with his drinking and his obsession with work. Fact was, it was his own fault. A year had passed, but the heartache remained. She lived with the Beaver Weaver fucker now and was working at the Launceston General Hospital. Wendy reckoned her mum was happy and part of him did not begrudge her that. The worst thing was that he would have to sell the Darcy Street house because the divorce settlement would be coming through soon. Such thoughts occupied Jack's mind as he picked his way down the street, taking care not to slip on the frost sparkling underfoot.

The Golden Dragon was doing a brisk takeaway trade. He was waiting to be shown to a table when a man emerged from the toilets and barged through the main doors to the street, knocking another customer aside with a muttered apology. Jack did a double take and the hairs stood up on the back of his neck. The man was the spitting image of Gordon Paisley, but then he couldn't be, Jack reflected, because the former detective sergeant was serving a life sentence for murder in Risdon Prison. Still, the bloke had the same moon face and the Dennis Lillee moustache sported by Jack's unloved former colleague. The same boof head and squat body as that one he thought of as the Human Toad.

A quick call to the prison the next day eased Jack's mind but left him puzzled. Paisley was still in special confinement with the sex offenders—the regular crims took a dim view of kiddie fiddlers and defrocked coppers. 'Once a copper, always a copper,' his snout Ernie Dark had once ventured in his cups. Four of the Nazis were out, however, and they would need to follow that up. He'd get Bluey onto it.

Jack ate at the Chinese restaurant most nights that week, but the man didn't return. Commander Holmes allowed Jack to go home to Darcy Street, but insisted on regular patrols of the neighbourhood. Glaziers had replaced the kitchen window with bulletproof glass and Duncan Snodgers had finished sweeping the place for clues. It was good to be home, but Jack slept with his service pistol under the pillow at Commander Holmes's insistence. Despite this unpleasantness, he was delighted to learn that Wendy was coming home soon. She had quarrelled with her Yank boyfriend, Milton Otis Orgreave-Clothier III—what kind of name was that, for Christ's sake—and had decided to come home and finish her degree. The boyfriend had headed north from Valparaiso, muttering about hitchhiking back to the States. Jack hoped that he had gone for good. Wendy had gone out with a communist once and a boy racer type before that and ratbags though they were, they were more acceptable than the Milton Otis Orgreave-Clothier III waster. The *Third*, for Christ's sake, Jack sneered. He had a vision of an assembly line in Detroit turning out little Orgreave-Clothiers and sending them round the world as ambassadors for Uncle Sam. At least there would never be a Milton Otis Orgreave-Clothier IV with *his* daughter. He went to work whistling that 'suicide is painless' song and got Bluey to check up to see if any of the Nazis were out of prison.

There was a grubby manilla envelope posted at the Hobart GPO on his desk. The note inside was written in the laboured script of the poorly educated, in capital letters and with numerous blots and scratchings-out:

YOUR A BASTARD MARTIN SO YOU ARE. YOU KNOW WHAT YOU DONE. I AM YOUR WURST NIHGTMARE YOU BETTER BELEIVE IT, SAY YOUR PRARES YOU MAKE ME BOAK SO YOU DO. YOUR TIME IS UP YOU HALLION SO IT IS

Duncan Snodgers found no fingerprints and the paper and envelope were widely available cheap stuff. Jack refused to move back to the police safe house, so Derek Holmes insisted on stationing an armed officer in his house around the clock. This crap would need cleaning up before Wendy got back.

***

Around this time, there was a spate of bashings in Hobart. A young man was found wandering bloodied and dazed near the rivulet in South Hobart. A jogger had seen him crawling out of the stream and called an ambulance, but the man had hobbled off into the bush by the time it arrived. Fuller and Langdale speculated that the assault was part of a war between rival drug gangs. A young man answering the victim's description had been hanging around the local primary school and the teachers believed he was attempting to sell drugs to the kids. It was either gang warfare or vigilantes, but the detectives could find no evidence of the latter and nobody had claimed responsibility. More outrages followed. Another young man was rescued from a dinghy set adrift in the ship channel underneath the Tasman Bridge. There were no oars or motor and he had been tied up after a serious beating. His name was Scott Harrison and he had no form. There were reports, too, of fights in back streets and two young men had set on each other with knives outside Ogilvie High School. Another young man had been slashed with razors and only just made it to Emergency. If apprehended, none of them would talk.

'You wouldn't read about it,' said Sergeant Fuller when they met in the canteen. He helped himself to some sausage rolls and sauce. 'Bloke was found in the Elizabeth Street Mall early this morning. Freezing bloody cold, but he'd been stripped naked and tied to one of them steel benches. Someone had given him a good hiding too, and I think he'd been pistol-whipped.'

'Who was it?' Jack asked, his hand hovering between the sausage rolls and a tuna salad. Eeny meeny ... he felt virtuous when he took the salad. Fuller sniggered. He reckoned Jack couldn't keep up the health kick.

'Ha. It was that tosser Jason Toomey. No convictions, but we've had our eyes on him for a while now.' He took a big bite from his sausage roll and continued, spraying the table with pastry crumbs. 'He's mixed up with the Mitropoulos firm. Looks like some other mob is taking over.'

'Ah,' said Jack, nibbling on his salad. 'Maybe he's losing

his grip a bit after a few years of running his firm from inside the Pink Palace. Tell you what though, Mitropoulos is a vicious creep. If this new mob are taking on Mitropoulos and winning, they must be deadly.'

The war continued, but the police had no clues as to who the new mob were.

CHAPTER 5

THE FOLLOWING SUNDAY Jack drove to the Cornelian
Bay cemetery at the northern edge of the Domain, the green
belt between the river and the inner northern suburbs. It was
a melancholy place, but beautiful for all that. Jack loved the
city on days such as this. The river was black and calm, the
air still and with just enough warmth to make it pleasant,
although the deep shadows underneath the trees were chill
and damp. Driving there, he had taken in the houses on the
steep hillsides and marvelled the city's guardian mountain
rising high behind them to the flutes of the Organ Pipes.
Surely there were few cities in the world blessed with such a
stunning location.

Little knots of mourners were milling about at the cemetery, their voices sharp on the winter air, and Jack's heart filled
with the soft melancholy that graveyards engender. There was
beauty in the cypress trees, the simple headstones, the rearing
crosses, the dark estuary, the smell of new-mown grass, and
the great humped mass of the mountain behind it all—but it
was also a place of sorrow. Clutching three bunches of flowers
and a garden trowel, Jack went first to where the remains of
his old friend and colleague Damien Mazengarb slept under
a Celtic cross. Someone had pinched the vase, so he replaced

it with one from a grave at a discreet distance. Mazengarb had been killed in a car chase years ago, with Jack at the wheel, and the guilt hung heavy over him still, although an inquiry had absolved him of blame. A quick clean-up of the weeds and he moved on to where his father lay under a headstone with the inscription,

ALDO MARTINUZZI

BORN TRIESTE ITALY 23 APRIL 1925

DIED HOBART 18 JULY 1948

BELOVED HUSBAND OF DAWN

PROUD FATHER OF GIACOMO

Jack had paid a stonemason to add the words HE FOUGHT AND DIED FOR FREEDOM.

Jack missed his dad though he'd never known him. Aldo had emigrated after the war and found work as a carpenter on the Tasmanian hydro dams. During the war, he had fought with the partisans against Nazis and Blackshirts in his native Istria. One snowy winter's evening, a fascist called Roman Ferenczak had ambushed him in a laneway off Salamanca Place down by Sullivan's Cove. Jack regretted not reverting to his proper Italian surname, but it was perhaps too late now, and only a few people remembered him as Giacomo Martinuzzi, the Queenstown golden boy whose mother had succumbed to alcoholism. Recently, he'd enrolled in an Italian language class at TAFE, anxious to make up to his father's shade.

Next, Jack took the trowel and the remaining bunch of roses and wandered across to where Lily Ferenczak's remains lay under a baroque Catholic confection. Lily had been his first love. He placed the roses tenderly in the vase on the grave and ran his hand over the trite, but well-meant inscription on the headstone. Her Slovenian *Volksdeutsche* mother had been a good woman; her Ukrainian father a fascist beast whom Jack suspected of war crimes. Tasmania was far away from the conflicts of old Europe in terms of physical distance but the mass migration of peoples to Australia after the war had brought them closer and they cast a long shadow over Jack's life. He often wondered what it would have been like had his father survived the attack in the alleyway. He was proud of his dad and now, in middle age, was anxious to re-connect with his language and culture.

He stood for a while lost in thought and his mind went back as it often did to Lily. She was the most beautiful girl and woman he had ever known, both in terms of her looks and her nature. Alas, she had taken her own life. Her husband had beaten her. The Church had failed her. Her father, Roman, had killed Jack's father Aldo and many others besides and in the end had blown his own head off with a shotgun. Only an elderly priest's compassion had saved Lily's family from the disgrace of burying her as well as her father in unhallowed ground. If the priest had sinned, Jack reckoned the deity should forgive him. He had read Lily's obituary in Soroka's Queenstown café, which made it harder to bear for it was in that West Coast mining town that he had fallen in love with her, lost her, met her again, and then lost her for good when she retreated into herself.

Grey clouds billowed down off the mountain and smothered the thin winter sun. Wendy was due home in a few days though, and that gave his heart a lift. When she left, she hadn't been sure when—or if—she would come home. At one stage she was considering living in the States with Orgreave-Clothier III and although Jack wanted her to be independent the news had hit him like a physical blow, and he realised he had grieved badly. Shivering in his thin jacket, Jack squared his shoulders and headed back along the paths through the gravestones. Wrapped in his thoughts, he took little note of the figure watching from a thicket of trees just outside the cemetery gates.

Jack's feeling of contentment was short-lived. As he was driving towards the Brooker Highway, a large black four-wheel drive, its driver hidden by tinted windows, suddenly sideswiped his Holden Commodore. Jack spun the steering wheel frantically, but his car careered off the road and slammed into a large gum tree. The bonnet flew open with a loud bang and the airbag inflated in less than half the blinking of an eye. Jack wrestled the billowing folds from his face only to see the other vehicle drive off with a roar of exhaust, its tinted windows hiding the driver. There'd been no chance of seeing the number plate even if it had one. His door protested arthritically as he pushed it open and got out to survey the damage. Fuck. The radiator was steaming, and the bonnet had twisted into a pathetic grimace. His doctor had been pleased with his blood pressure but after this it would surely shoot back up again. He flexed his legs and rotated his head gingerly. At least he appeared to be uninjured, physically at least. He was getting bloody well sick of this.

CHAPTER 6

'NO, IT WAS NOT AN ACCIDENT,' Jack told Derek Holmes, shaking his head emphatically when they met the next day. 'It's a perfectly straight stretch of road with plenty of room to overtake. The bastard followed me from the cemetery gates, pulled out alongside and then deliberately forced me off the road.'

'He?' Holmes fixed Jack with his piercing green gaze.

'Yes, I'm afraid I was in another world, but I have a dim memory of a man standing near the cemetery gates, watching.'

Holmes ordered the guard doubled on Jack's house and arranged for the installation of hidden cameras around the Darcy Street property. Jack wondered again about the anonymous death threat. There was something about it that he couldn't quite put his finger on. The spelling and punctuation errors told him that a poorly educated person had written it, but there were clues that he was missing. Danny would know. Danny Cunningham was an associate professor in the English department at the university. They went way back to when Jack was a young plod and Danny was a regular in the same pub.

They met in the university refectory, and Jack saw that Danny hadn't changed much—he had been a scruff in his younger days, and he was still slopping around in an unironed work shirt with the tail hanging out over horrible baggy trousers made of some ancient, unidentifiable fabric. Jack recalled old blokes wearing such things in Queenstown when he was a boy. Danny was wearing a threadbare bluey coat too, just like the miners. The beard and mop of blond hair were grey now, but a pair of bottle-thick glasses were still perched on his pointed nose, smeared as ever, and there were dinner stains down his front. Jack ordered cappuccinos—*cappuccini*, Danny the pedant corrected—and they sat near the steamed-up windows, half watching a protest rally on the steps outside. Something to do with forests, as ever. Jack didn't blame them but kept his opinions to himself in the cop shop. Danny smoothed the folds from the photocopy on the table and raised his bushy eyebrows. Jack put on his spectacles and read the note again over Danny's shoulder. The man smelled of clothes that had never dried properly. That and pipe smoke.

YOUR A BASTARD MARTIN SO YOU ARE. YOU NO WHAT YOU DONE. I AM YOUR WURST NIHGTMARE YOU BETTER BELEIVE IT, SAY YOUR PRARES YOU MAKE ME BOAK SO YOU DO. YOUR TIME IS UP YOU HALLION SO IT IS

'It's written in a dialect of Hibernian English,' Danny pronounced, scratching his beard and dislodging a blizzard of dandruff, and launching into lecturing mode. 'In fact, I'd say it's an example of the sociolect spoken in one of the inner working-class suburbs of Belfast. They speak a hybrid in Northern Ireland, you know—a result of the Ulster Plantation back in the seventeenth century. It's an amalgam of Southwest Scots with Northern and Midlands English with the old Gaelic rhythms of speech.' Jack nodded. It made sense so far. 'Two unusual words here,' said Cunningham, pointing at the note. '"Boak" and "hallion". They're Scots words—boak meaning to vomit and hallion meaning a useless person. Then there's the repetitive phrasing for emphasis—"so you are", "so you do" and "so it is". It's a typical speech pattern from those parts, and in western Scotland. They would say, "she's my girlfriend, so she is"; "he's a Siamese cat, so he is"; "they love Guinness, so they do"; and so on. Your man is not aware of doing it. As for the accent, think the Reverend Ian Paisley'—here Danny did an impression of the old bigot ranting against the Pope as the Great Whore of Satan, much to the amusement of students at nearby tables. 'You know yourself that he's not well-educated. Either that or he's trying to put you off the scent, but I don't think so. It would take a considerable amount of calligraphic talent to mimic that uncouth handwriting … I hope that's helpful.'

'Well, it certainly narrows it down!' Jack joked. 'You've been a great help, Danny, and I owe you one.' After finishing their coffees and chatting a bit about old times, they went their separate ways, promising to catch up again before another decade had gone by. Maybe they even would. Jack felt a jolt of nostalgia, recalling the old days when they always seemed to be having fun, although he knew we tend to forget the other times. He decided to call in at Darcy Street on his way into the city and found another suspicious envelope among the bills and whatnot in the letterbox. Donning a pair of the latex gloves he carried in the glovebox of his police car, he carefully slit it open. Written in the same unlettered hand as the first note, it declared,

> I BEEN PLAYING WITH YOU CUNT BECASE
> YOU NEED TO SUFFER. DON'T WORRY ILL
> GET YOU SO I WILL

This time, Mrs Hitzenbichler was more helpful. 'It vos der same man in der red baseball cap,' she enthused. 'His auto I have der rego nummer for. A big black car and it parked on der udder side of the street und I saw it vos bashed in on von side. *Ja.* Der man's hair vos *dunkel*—dark, you know—und his head vos like zis'—here she indicated that it was very fat, 'like a pumpkin, *ja! Und*, oh yes, he had a big moustache on his face.'

The junior constables who were supposed to be keeping watch over Jack's house would be facing disciplinary charges. One had been asleep while the other was down at the milk bar in Macquarie Street buying cigarettes and coffee. He wanted to kick their arses into next week. A quick phone call found that the big black car was registered in the name of a Peter Cripps, who had reported it stolen early that morning. Mr Cripps, who lived alone in Lord Street, Sandy Bay, had been in Melbourne on an extended business trip. A jogger found it the next day burned out near McRobie's Gully in South Hobart.

Mrs Hitzenbichler's description of the man, plus Danny Cunningham's analysis of the first note, pointed towards a connection with Gordon Paisley; a hypothesis strengthened by Jack's fleeting encounter with the look-alike in the Golden Dragon. Fuller and Langdale interviewed Paisley's ex-wife Nancy but learned nothing new. Paisley had a sister, but she was living in Queensland, and the parents were dead. There were relatives back in Belfast, but Nancy had never met any of them. She had divorced Paisley following his trial and had remarried. She wanted nothing more to do with the family and her adult sons Pat and Eric felt the same way. Commander Holmes asked Immigration if anyone called Paisley had entered the country in recent weeks, but the reply when it finally came was negative. Meanwhile, Bluey reported that two Nazis had gone to Melbourne shortly after their release from prison. Their freedom had been short-lived. Arrested for peddling drugs outside a Footscray school, they were now doing time at Pentridge.

CHAPTER 7

JACK DROVE OUT TO THE AIRPORT to pick up Wendy and was relieved when she walked into Arrivals alone, without the obnoxious Milton Otis Orgreave-Clothier III. They had grown close in recent years and hugged with real affection. Gone was the prickly teenager and he had made a major effort to stop being judgemental—except about the Orgreave-Clothier fucker, but he kept quiet on that score. Wendy had grown into a fine young woman and Jack was proud of her. He owed her a lot. She had helped him to moderate his drinking and give up the cigarettes and after Helen left, she had insisted that he eat properly and stop moping. She had also suggested that he should see a psychologist.

Jack had reared up at that. 'What? Do you reckon I'm mad, now?'

She looked him coolly in the eye. 'Dad, you're a hard man in some ways, but if you continue to shut all the horror inside you, you really will go mad.' She didn't say that it had been a factor in her mother's decision to leave, but she didn't have to. He had to admit, too, that seeing the shrink had done him the world of good. He had come to realise that he was suffering from something akin to PTSD; that years of dealing with things nobody should ever have to see had taken their toll. Some of his colleagues—Fuller and Langdale for instance, even Liz Flakemore to a degree—could switch off but Jack never could. At least he no longer bottled it all up inside and didn't seek escape in self-harming behaviours. Dr Ziegler had suggested strategies for coping, and they were working most of the time.

Such was Jack's love that he had prepared a suitable vegetarian dinner for Wendy: a tofu and veggie curry with a few little side dishes, chutney, and the like. She praised his cooking and he had to admit that it didn't taste too bad at all despite the absence of dead animal bits. Wendy took some out to the constables doing guard duty and they gobbled it down like a pair of Labradors with Prader-Willi syndrome. Their boss, Inspector Aldridge, had given them a second chance and they were anxious to please. They were meat pie, steak and KFC men—'none o' that bloody rabbit food'—but they told each other 'this veggie stuff's real fuckin' good' and when Wendy went out for the dishes they asked for seconds. Mrs Hitzenbichler took them out a tray of *Apfelstrudel* and *Hutzelbrot* although she wasn't supposed to know they were there.

'*Kaffee* und *Kuchen*, boys,' she said, rapping on the car window. She almost called them *Kinder*, and they smiled their appreciation. '*Gott* knows,' she wondered, 'that dese babies are protecting *das Publikum* from der criminals.' They were truly artless, like big puppies.

Meanwhile, in a rented flat in a charmless yellow brick block out in West Moonah, a culinary atrocity was taking place. A stocky brown-haired man was trying to heat a tin of beans on a cranky electric hotplate. It was a mean abode, but he had lived in meaner, and mean suited him because he was a mean bastard. He gave up trying to coax and threaten the hotplate into life, shovelled the beans down cold and wiped the sauce from his moustache with his fingers. He would fix the fuckers, so he would, he muttered, squinting out into the winter night through the tatty nylon lace curtains. Over the road, in another brick box, a rake-thin brunette who called herself Jaymee-Lee Winchester was bidding a client goodnight at her front door. The client crept off, paranoid that the bishop would learn of his sins. 'The dirty wee hoor,' sneered the watcher, standing back when she glanced towards his window. 'And a man of the cloth at it with her, so he is.'

CHAPTER 8

THE NEXT MORNING, a shaven-headed young man drove back to Taroona from the supermarket in Sandy Bay, where he'd stocked up on smokes and booze. He saw the flashing blue lights in the side street just in time and kept driving straight ahead along the Channel Highway towards the Shot Tower. He didn't think the coppers had twigged him. Looked like the game was up. The job had been shitting him anyway; it was easy money, but it was as boring as Launceston on a wet Sunday afternoon. Sitting there day in day out watching TV when he could have been in the pub or rooting Maxine, was driving him stir-crazy. Fuckin' pigs. Now he'd have to drive round the long way through Kingston and leave a message for Mr Sokolov and the driver to stay away. He kept looking in the rear vision mirror and kept strictly to the speed limit but there was no sign of coppers in pursuit. He didn't think he had left anything compromising in the house. That Sokolov feller, the Russian wog, had always been going on about that. Pain in the arse, but not the sort of bloke you would cross, though Baldy fancied himself as a hard man. A thought struggled to jell in the thick grey sludge of his brain—if that stupid bitch Maxine had opened her gob, there would be hell to pay. Fuck, he thought. Left me jacket on the chair. Too late now!

Jack had received the message shortly after arriving at the station that morning. A young female had rung in sounding frazzled: *'I can't stand it no more! You gotta get down there an' get them kids outta that place!'* She had given an address in Taroona and then hung up after refusing to give her name. The tech people had traced the call to a public phone box in Elizabeth Street just north of the CBD, but she was long gone.

Jack acted swiftly. The Shipstern horror was never far from his thoughts so the mention of kids in peril sent alarm bells ringing in his head. Taroona is normally fifteen minutes south from the CBD by car, but it took his team a fraction of that time with a carload of uniformed police close behind, tyres smoking, lights flashing and sirens wailing. The cavalry in full cry. They hurtled past St David's Park, screamed through a red light at St George's Terrace, and clocked 90 kilometres an hour past the cylinder of the casino on the Sandy Bay waterfront. Heads spun round as they roared into Taroona, an affluent suburb perched between forested hills and the broad Derwent estuary. The house the woman had rung about was a large single-storey red brick place halfway down a leafy cul-de-sac near the river. The grounds were overgrown and the house uncared for, with peeling paint and grimy windows: a stark contrast with its sedate surroundings. It was on a double block and isolated from its neighbours by thick hedges, with enough trees out the back to qualify as a small orchard, although they too were unkempt.

'Impressive house,' said Liz Flakemore as she parked the

car. 'Not like the off-the-shelf boxes they throw up these days.'

They opened the front gate, brushing aside the dead leaves blowing this way and that in the wind, and Liz and Bluey went to investigate round the back while Jack pounded on the front door. There was no response, but he sensed there were people inside the house. A quick check of the fuse box showed that the electricity was on. Blinds and thick curtains covered all the windows, which were locked shut. Another car arrived and Constable Kate Farrar jumped out, bright and keen-eyed.

'Sir, Inspector Martin,' she puffed, proud and anxious. 'Place is owned by Taurus Holdings ...' She consulted her notebook. 'It's a Melbourne firm, sir. They lease it to a Mr Scott Taylor, whose address is a North Hobart post office box. Taylor pays cash regularly every six months but nobody at Taurus has met him. The receptionist reckons he uses an intermediary.' She paused again before continuing, while Jack stood by looking slightly bemused. 'This Taylor has leased the place for two years since the old bloke who owned it died. A Mr Donald Crosthwaite.'

They checked the letterbox, which had bills spilling out, all of them addressed to Crosthwaite.

When repeated knocking failed to elicit any response, and Liz and Bluey found the back door locked, Jack signalled to the waiting constables to bring the 'enforcer'. Two burly officers stepped up, counted to two and swung the 'big red key' at the door on the third count. The enforcer bounced back. Most doors splintered easily but this one was unusually sturdy, and it took another three blows before the lock gave up. Someone had reinforced the door with steel plate, and someone had been there recently: a cup of instant coffee standing on the kitchen bench was still tepid. The kitchen was tidy enough, but it stank of cigarette smoke and someone's feet. A denim jacket was draped over the back of a chair. They would bag it. Whoever lived here had not made the effort to make it anything more than functional, but it was a truly beautiful house, with dark wood wainscoting and ornamental plaster ceilings. There were no books. No records. No magazines. Just a large television set in the lounge room. An ashtray overflowed next to a pair of tatty armchairs facing the box. Lots of DNA there too. There were six bedrooms but only one showed any signs of recent occupation, with a ratty old sleeping bag and a greasy pillow without a case draped on the bed. Looked like a used condom. There were some unused ones on a bedside table.

'A bum steer?' Bluey suggested. 'Don't look like there's nothing here.'

Jack frowned at the grammar but let it slide. 'Something's definitely not right,' he replied, donning latex gloves and reaching up to begin opening the first of a long line of kitchen cupboards. Someone had slammed it shut to stop the contents from falling out—leaning towers of plastic cups, plates, and bowls. The next one contained dozens of cans of cheap baked beans and spaghetti, packets of instant soup and suchlike. Other cupboards contained stashes of sugary breakfast cereal—Grinners, Coco Pops, Frosties and Fruit Loops—stuff he'd banned in his house when Wendy was little. A freezer hummed quietly in one corner, full of loaves of sliced white bread. Jack wrenched open the fridge door and saw that although it was dirty, it was stocked with milk cartons, margarine, and packaged plastic cheese. There was a huge green rubbish bin in the corner, stinking of cigarette butts and full of empty cans, milk cartons, paper plates, plastic cutlery, and dead Jim Beam bottles.

'Whaddyacall them people in America who stockpile food and that?' asked Bluey.

'Survivalists,' Jack replied. 'but they'd eat better than this. Anyway, I want Duncan Snodgers down here pronto and everything bagged.'

Liz Flakemore came in just then and reported that there didn't seem to be anything of interest in the garden shed. Just old gardening tools and junk that the real estate people hadn't got around to throwing out. 'There's been a bit of digging, though,' she said thoughtfully. 'Funny because whoever lives here definitely isn't the gardening type.' She gave Jack a meaningful look.

There was also a large garage, accessible through a door in the hall. There was no car, but the roller door appeared to be in good nick and there was a lingering whiff of exhaust fumes as if it had been used recently. The thing was, though, that there was no sign of the kids the woman had been so concerned about.

'Carpets,' thought Jack, noticing his shoes sunk into the stuff—a thick, good quality English Axminster import if he wasn't wrong, but the edges were not tacked down. He paced slowly down the corridor, stamping his feet, convinced that there must be kids underneath. Halfway down the hallway, the floor sounded hollow underfoot. He peeled up the carpet. Aha! There, cut professionally into the Tasmanian oak floor-boards, was a trapdoor with a brass latch. He bent to lift it, but it refused to budge and upon closer inspection, Jack saw that there was a mortise lock recessed into the wood.

'Bring the biggest bloody pinch bar you can find!' he shouted. 'Here, quickly!'

A minute or so later a young constable he knew as Barney arrived bearing a pinch bar in one hand and a crowbar in the other. Barney set to work with the smaller tool, but he couldn't get enough leverage. He dropped it and attacked the gap between the trapdoor and the side of the hatch with the crowbar. The lock gave and the trapdoor groaned open reluctantly.

'Good man,' said Jack, peering into the hole. He recoiled as fetid air wafted up.

'Shit!' said Barney, covering his nose.

'Torch here, quick as you can,' Jack ordered, ignoring the smell.

When Barney returned, Jack took the torch and began to descend the ladder into the cavity below. At the bottom, seven feet below the floorboards, there was a light switch at the side of the ladder. Jack flicked it on and turned slowly round before closing his eyes and muttering a half-forgotten prayer to the Virgin Mary. At the other side of the rough-hewn cellar, six kids—boys and girls—were huddled together against the wall, regarding him with huge eyes.

'Police,' Jack said softly. 'You're safe now.'

His words did nothing to reassure them. They crouched closer together and one of them began to cry—a high-pitched keening sound that cut Jack to the bone. Half of the dirt floor of the cellar was covered in thin mattresses, over which sleeping bags were strewn. The stench came from slop buckets overflowing in the corner.

'Liz!' he called. 'Liz, get down here fast as you can!' Jack crouched down and held out his hands to the kids. 'You're safe,' he repeated. 'Police. The bad people can't hurt you anymore.'

The kids shrank back, terrified.

Liz descended the ladder nimbly behind him, took one look and made her way over to the children. They cringed but one of them—a girl of maybe 13 or 14—shuffled towards Liz and fell into her arms. By this time, Barney and Bluey had descended the ladder and were standing with horrified expressions frozen on their faces. The children were babbling in a foreign language, but one of them with a smattering of English seemed to be telling the others they were safe. '*Polici. Milicija,*' she said.

Jack called up to the sergeant who was peering down from the trapdoor to call an ambulance, bring plenty of blankets and get an interpreter pronto. The children sounded like they might be from the Balkans, so Jack added that a Serbo-Croatian speaker would be best.

Meanwhile, the uniformed constables had fanned out door to door along the street. Most of the residents seemed to be at work but a woman in a house opposite had a lot to say. Mrs Justine Corfield had a permanently indignant expression on her thin face and once she got going it was difficult to inter-rupt her flow. 'It all went downhill when poor Mr Crosthwaite died,' she told Constable Kate Farrar. 'I've only seen the new people once or twice and I didn't like the look of them.'

'Why not?' asked Kate.

'Ooh, I can't really say for sure, but they were … unsavoury. Something not right about them. They didn't seem to really live there. Like they were camping. If you ask me, they're gangsters. Nasty types.' She stopped and shuddered. 'There were always comings and goings late at night. A big black car would drive up. Sorry, I'm no good with the makes, but it was a big sedan. Black or dark blue, maybe. Sometimes, too, I thought I heard children crying, but I've never seen any kids there since Mr Crosthwaite's grandchildren stopped coming.'

Thank God for curtain-twitchers, thought Kate, scribbling this all down in her notebook. 'You've been very helpful Mrs Corfield.'

The constables taped off the house and garden. Duncan Snodgers shambled down the front path, wiping his brow despite the chill in the air, and ordering everyone 'oot o' the hoose!' Social workers arrived and took the children away in a large ambulance, wrapped in blankets.

Jack and Liz by this time were standing in the back garden, studying the patch of turned earth. 'If you're thinking what I'm thinking,' said Liz, her big green eyes pools of sadness, 'we'll have to get Duncan and his team out here to dig that lot up.'

'Yep,' sighed Jack. 'I don't think they've been planting spuds.'

CHAPTER 9

YOU DID NOT CONTRADICT MR SOKOLOV. Not ever. One look from those colourless eyes and Baldy knew to keep his trap shut. Sokolov could have been from anywhere. He had an accent that Baldy thought was Russian although he 'didn't know nothing about foreign places.' There was something military about Sokolov. He was somewhere in his 40s, with a muscular frame honed to a fighting finish in the gym. He had a hard, bony face, with a long scar running down one side, and if you looked too long into those eyes you had that feeling that someone was walking over your grave, the bald one believed. Baldy had considered himself a tough guy until he met Sokolov, even done a bit of cage fighting over in Melbourne. Been a bouncer in clubs, strip clubs and Mrs Moran's brothels. Sokolov reminded him of that video he'd watched with Maxine. 'Blade Runner it was called,' he reminded her. 'The one with them replingcunts or whatever they was called innit. Anyway, this Sokolov bloke has got steel teeth!' Sokolov had seen him looking once and said yeah, they're finest Damascus steel. Chew a man's throat out just like that. Done it too against the Mujahideen, whoever they was.

Baldy had driven round the long way from Taroona and reported straightaway to Sokolov that the coppers had turned up at the house. Sokolov wasn't pleased and Baldy almost begged him to please don't shoot the messenger.

Sokolov looked at him for a good minute before he spoke in that gravelly voice. 'How they know?' he demanded.

He didn't raise his voice. Didn't need to; scare the pants off you, he would. Sokolov waited for an answer, still and calm as the lake when Baldy was fishing years ago up at Bronte with his dad. He wished he could go back there.

'Jeez, Mr Sokolov, I d-dunno. Honest I d-don't,' he said, the words tumbling off his tongue. 'First thing I knew was they w-was all over the street outside the house …' His voice petered out to a croak.

'Well, someone tipped cops over,' said Sokolov, 'and better not be you. Now, take black car and drive to Glenorchy. Tell Custard to get his fat arse in here quickly smart. Stay there. Now, fuck off.'

Sokolov jerked his head towards the door and the bald man fled, too scared to wipe the look of relief off his face. He felt Sokolov's eyes boring into his back all the way out to the car.

When Baldy got out to the place in Glenorchy, Custard Sproule peered at him through the peephole and took his time about opening up. Always was cack-handed, was Custard, so he fiddled with the locks until Baldy wanted to scream and punch something. The house was like any one of a thousand out near Tolosa Street—an ageing white-painted weatherboard with a couple of tree ferns down the side and a bit of lawn out the front. It was built on the side of a hill, which meant there was a big rumpus room underneath. Custard was still in his pyjamas and had a cigarette stuck in his mouth.

'Whaddya want, Les?' he mumbled. Custard was a grotty bastard, with dirty hair and grimy hands and anything you said went straight back to Sokolov even though they was supposed to be mates.

'Boss reckons you gotta get yer fat arse back an' I gotta stay 'ere.'

'Woffor?' Custard demanded, stubbing his cigarette on the door jamb, and throwing it into the yard. He didn't move. Just stood there scratching his balls. Les—Baldy—shrugged and brushed past him into the house. He rinsed out one of the dirty mugs Custard had left on the sink and made himself a cup of instant coffee. Lucky I stocked up on smokes and booze, he thought. Meanwhile, Custard had put on a pair of holey tracksuit pants and a T-shirt and was looking at him with his glassy eyes as he laced up his runners.

''Ow's them below?' Les asked, stirring his coffee and nodding towards the basement.

'One of 'em's a bit crook,' replied Custard, still scratching his crotch. 'I give her some Panadol, but the cow just lies there an' moans.'

'Well, ya better tell Sokolov when ya get back,' Les advised. 'He's gunna go apeshit if we lose another one.'

'Well, I ain't no doctor,' Custard blustered. 'Done me best.'

Les had wandered over to the TV and was surfing through the channels. 'See ya,' he said over his shoulder as Custard went out the door. Maybe he'd risk bringing Maxine here. Send her out the back if that cunt Sokolov come round.

CHAPTER 10

'OK, EVERYBODY LISTEN NOW!' Jack commanded, clapping his hands together to get the troops' attention. The shuffling, fidgeting, head nodding and animated conversations around the incident room petered out. 'Thank you,' he said. 'Now that we're sitting comfortably, we can begin.' He paused and looked at his notes. 'What we have is six young teenagers—three boys and three girls—rescued this morning from a house in Taroona.' He stopped and signalled for Bluey Bishop to stick six blown-up photographs up on the whiteboard. 'We attended the crime scene after an anonymous tip-off. The caller refused to give her name and as she made the call from a public call box, we don't know who she is. The interpreter, Stefan Jovanović, has ascertained that the kids come from Kosovo—that's in the south of what used to be Yugoslavia in case you're wondering.

'One more thing to bear in mind is that the boy who died on Shipstern Bluff some months back was of Balkan appearance. It's just speculation but we can't rule out a connection.' Here, Jack invited Liz Flakemore to continue.

'As Jack says,' said Liz, taking up the story, 'the six youngsters are from Kosovo and we believe some are ethnic Albanians and some are Serbs. They are all aged in their early teens—the oldest is barely 15 and the youngest is 12. They told Stefan that "bad men" took them from their villages during the fighting, but they are vague on the details of how they came to be here. The bad men were Albanian, but they passed the kids on to others. The kids were on a ship at some stage and in the back of trucks for another part of the journey. Even it seems on an aeroplane, apparently over Bass Strait. I'm afraid that they have lost track of how long they were kept in the cellar at Taroona, but it seems we are talking of weeks rather than days. The conditions they were kept in were horrible.' Here, Liz paused, drank some water, and steeled herself to continue.

'They've been fed on cheap tinned food, packet soups and bread. The lavatory facilities were disgusting—a line of buckets along one wall with a subsidiary hatch up through which one of the bad men'—here she made air quotes—'hauled the buckets when they were full. It seems that the bad man who was usually in the house only speaks English and often wears a denim jacket—we've got that for forensic analysis and there's a great deal of other stuff that Duncan will be examining. The man has a shaven head and although he shouted at the kids, he never hit them. Smelled strongly of alcohol. He never gave his name. Usually had stubble but not a beard. They called him Baldy among themselves—it's the same word in Albanian and Serbo-Croatian, apparently. As soon as we can, we'll get an identikit of Baldy made. The sleeping arrangements were primitive—thin rubber mattresses and Kmart sleeping bags.

The kids had to huddle together against the cold because there was no heating and very little ventilation.' Liz paused again to drink some more water and ran her hand through her short blonde hair. She was visibly distressed, so Jack smiled reassuringly and told her to take her time.

'Now, the story gets worse,' Liz continued. 'I'm afraid that these kids have been trafficked for sex … Sometimes the men took them at night in a big black car to another place where other men in masks would sexually abuse them. We are talking of rape and enslavement of minors here. The kids have no idea where this place is. In fact, they had no idea that they were in Tasmania. The car would park round the back of a big stone building and the men would hustle them inside. We know that the kids could understand a bit of what some of the bad men were saying, so we are thinking perhaps they are Russian or some other Slavic nationality. The place had thick carpets and tall windows through which they could see what we think must have been the city lights. There was a bar, with men drinking and others were sitting round in big armchairs. They all had masks on. None of these men spoke Serbian or Albanian and the kids say they were all old—although that could be any age over 30, maybe. They would take the kids into smaller rooms to … to do what they did to them.'

The troops were silent. Liz signalled that she had finished, and Jack took over.

'The children have been taken into care,' he said. 'They have been examined by a doctor and physically they should recover from their ordeal. Psychologically is another matter. We have to tread softly here but we will glean everything we can from them about those who have trafficked and abused them.

'Now, a few more things before we get out and find these scumbags. Duncan Snodgers and his team are going through the place with fine-tooth combs as we speak. The place is full of DNA evidence because these bastards thought they were too clever to get caught. We shall be matching it painstakingly to see if we can find a match among the lowlifes of this city. As Liz says, when the kids are ready, we will get identikits of the men done and circulated ... Now any questions?'

The young constable whom Jack knew as Barney raised his hand. 'I'm Junior Constable Barney Hurst,' he said. 'I was assigned to the unit that raided the house. I noticed someone had been digging in what was otherwise an overgrown back garden. I'm wondering what it might mean.'

'Good question, Constable Hurst,' Jack replied. 'Duncan Snodgers has been briefed to investigate and we'll keep the team up to speed when and if that turns up anything.' Jack had a bad feeling about the patch of bare earth but did not want to speculate at this stage.

Kate Farrar asked, 'Did any of the kids escape, or try to?'

'The children tell us that a couple of them did try to escape, but that other men such as the one from the house were standing guard to stop them,' Jack replied. 'There seem to have been more kids at various stages, but I can't speculate about what that means.'

There were no other questions, so he said, 'Now, I know that all of us want to get out there and find these bastards, so I'll hand you over to DS Bishop, who will allocate your tasks. Oh, and the higher-ups have authorised all the overtime necessary to catch the offenders.'

The investigation team set to work with grim enthusiasm. Officers went door to door around Taroona until well into the evening questioning residents—unfortunately without learning anything beyond what Mrs Corfield had been able to provide. Other officers visited all the city's known sex offenders and others spoke with their informers. It was painstaking work and largely frustrating. Nobody knew anything, or they weren't saying, but the team kept at it doggedly. Meanwhile, Jack fronted a media conference.

After Jack had given a report to the assembled reporters, Chuck Laineux was the first to raise a hand. 'Inspector,' Chuck drawled, 'is there any connection between the Taroona case and that of the unfortunate young man whose body you found at Shipstern Bluff? Incidentally, has there been any progress on that particular case?'

Jack gave Chuck a hard stare. The old fox could be relied on to spin anything he said, so he chose his words carefully. 'Everything is possible, Chuck,' he replied. 'Given the circumstances, we can't rule out a connection, but we aren't making any assumptions. We will go about our investigations painstakingly until we find the culprits. Regarding your second question, I can only say that our inquiries are continuing, and we welcome any information that members of the public can provide.'

After the press briefing finished, Jack went to his office hoping to hear something from Duncan Snodgers. There was nothing, but he knew that Duncan refused to hurry. He turned to a stack of paperwork that was clogging up his in-tray. Bumph most of it, concocted by pencil-pushers to turn everyone else into one of their kind. He sighed and skimmed through the one on the top. It informed him that his report on crime statistics was seriously overdue. He contemplated throwing it in the round filing cabinet in the corner but realised that he would have to do it. The next one was headed 'Annual Report'. It meant that he would have to go through each monthly report to find the figures then insert these into the annual report. God knows where the old monthly reports were. Why couldn't the bureaucrats do it themselves? he wondered. His mood was darkening by the minute.

A knock on the door interrupted his musings. Before he could answer, Bluey Bishop shot into the room, all legs and flared nostrils, his breathing ragged and his red hair dishevelled. 'Sir!' he wheezed. 'Word ... just in that someone's ... blown up your car!'

Jack's blue eyes flashed. 'Blown up? My fucking car?' he roared.

'Yairs, sir. Someone blew it to the shithouse!'

'What about Wendy?' Jack demanded, already grabbing his coat. 'Anyone hurt?'

'It was Wendy, your daughter, who phoned in. She's in a bit of a state, but not injured. Liz Flakemore's gone up to help.'

Jack was already halfway out of the door, pulling on his coat. He'd get one of the constables to drop him off at Darcy Street. This was getting thoroughly out of hand. When he got home, he saw bits of his Holden Commodore strewn up and down the street. Its carcass was still smoking away, polluting the winter air with a burning plastic stink. Uniformed officers had sealed off the area and were keeping gawkers at bay. Liz Flakemore was talking with Mrs Hitzenbichler in the old lady's driveway. Liz raised a hand in greeting, but Jack rushed round the back and found Kate Farrar consoling Wendy. Wendy assured him that she was unharmed, and he gave her a big hug. She had just got back from seeing her old course coordinator at the university and had sat down with a cup of coffee when there was a loud bang—a kind of roaring bang—and then she had heard more smaller bangs, as bits of Jack's car were landing on the road. Norman had fled. The important thing, Jack thought, was that Wendy was unhurt and that nobody else had been injured. His concern turned to cold rage when he thought back over the series of incidents in which some maniac was trying to hurt and intimidate him. The constables keeping watch had been pulled off to take part in the search for clues in the Taroona case.

There was a knock on the front door. Liz Flakemore and Commander Holmes were standing on the porch and he stood aside to let them in. When they were sitting round the kitchen table with coffee, Jack remarked that he was going to get whoever it was.

Derek Holmes put up a cautionary hand. 'No Jack,' he said firmly. 'You're too close to this to be objective. Liz here will head up the investigation. Until we find the culprit, she will be off the Taroona investigation and on this full time.'

Jack shrugged irritably, but he could see the wisdom and Holmes continued. 'Besides, you already have your hands full with the Taroona case and we can't allow the Shipstern murder business to stall completely.' He paused to take a sip of the coffee the young constable had brewed. It passed muster. 'The second thing is that you and Wendy can't stay here until we solve this thing.' Jack tried to interrupt but he continued. 'There's no argument Jack. It's an order. Now, I can understand that you don't want to stay in that ratty little place out in Moonah. The wife and I have a two-bedroom flat under our place. The previous tenants moved out last week, so it's yours as long as you need it.'

'Norman too?' asked Jack.

'Norman? Oh, the cat. Yes, Norman too if you must. I want the pair of you to pack up immediately, and Constable Farrar here will drive you over.'

Liz Flakemore smiled. 'I'll get him for you, Jack. You can bet on that.' Jack believed her. She was a competent officer. Could be a driven one, and they were good friends. He would stay away from the case and leave her to it.

CHAPTER 11

MAXINE FOWLER! The big redheaded girl's face suddenly swam up into Jack's mind's eye as he was surfacing from REM sleep. He could hear her voice too. For a moment, he wondered where he was then it came back ... Someone had blown up his car ... He was in the granny flat under Derek Holmes's house over the river in Lindisfarne ... Wendy was safe in the next bedroom ... Norman was tugging at his sleeve and miaowing ... She could use the kitty litter tray ... What? *Maxine Fowler!* The voice on the recording: '*I can't stand it no more! You gotta get down there an' get them kids outta that place!*' It was hers. His brain cleared—the cogs had been whirling away while he slept and had unearthed the information lurking just beyond his conscious mind. Now it all came back. Five years ago, Maxine Fowler was a 15-year-old girl with a child's mind inside a woman's body; easy meat for whoever wanted to exploit her. She was probably the most ignorant person Jack had ever met—she believed that tap water was made in factories, that the earth was 'flat with bumps on it' and had never heard of the Hydro—and all this almost 130 years after Tasmania became the first Australian colony to introduce compulsory schooling. Whether she had ever been to school was a good question. She had run away from home up near Falmouth to escape a violent father and after sleeping rough in an old steam crane down at Constitution Dock, she had shacked up with a Nazi calling himself Horse Whistle—real name Darryl Cooke, and the idiot meant Horst Wessel. Five years ago, Jack had put Cooke in the Pink Palace as an accessory to murder, and Maxine had been fostered. She would be 19 or 20 now, and free to go her own way. Alas, some other unsavoury bastard must be taking advantage of her. Jack would run it past Liz Flakemore, who was running the investigation into the firebombing, as there could well be a connection between the two cases.

Jack found Liz in her office late that morning and they wandered down to the Domino café in Elizabeth Street for lunch. Of all his colleagues, Liz was the only one he could really call a friend. Fuller and Langdale were old acquaintances but he'd scarcely share a confidence with them.

'Yeah, I remember Maxine Fowler,' said Liz, pushing a wayward piece of eggplant back into her vegetarian focaccia. 'She was in that place in Swan Street with those master race specimens. I kept an eye on her for a bit afterwards.' She paused for a mouthful of coffee, dabbed her mouth with a serviette, and continued. 'It was a bloody depressing story I can tell you. She was pregnant at the time and the baby was adopted. She went into care but ran away when the bloke in the house came onto her. It happened a couple of times. The social workers got her into a remedial literacy course at the TAFE, but she ran away again because the same thing happened in the new house. When she turned 18, she went her own way. She was nicked for shoplifting a year or so ago and put on a good behaviour bond. I heard she went to Melbourne after that.' Liz finished her focaccia and pushed the plate to one side.

'Well, she's definitely back,' Jack said, finishing his last toasted sandwich. 'I've always been good with voices. I listened to the recording again and there is no doubt it's her. Track her down and we will be close to finding the bastards who are trafficking the kids.'

'And you reckon there could be a connection with the shooting and firebombing?'

'Maybe. If anyone has it in for me, it would be Maxine's old Nazi friends. Anyway, we'll have to pull out all the stops to find her and see if there is a connection.'

They ordered two more coffees and exchanged news about what they'd been doing.

'Marg says hello,' said Liz. 'Says she'd quite fancy you if she wasn't, you know.'

'Liar,' said Jack, but he was smiling.

Liz was finally going to graduate with first class honours in sociology, and she made Jack promise to come to the ceremony. Of course, he said, and meant it. With her brains Liz would go far up the hierarchy. She was a working-class girl made good by dint of her own drive and intelligence. Her first home had been a dreadful slum in Condell Place, North Hobart—a squalid terrace long since pulled down for a supermarket car park. Her biological father was a German sailor who had jumped ship, got her mother pregnant, then vanished. Her mum had met a decent chap after that, and they had lived uneventfully in the Goodwood housing estate. If she didn't fancy staying in the police there would be a career for her as an academic, of that Jack was certain and he'd told her so often enough.

'Anyway, enough about me,' Liz said. 'What have you been up to, apart from being shot at and firebombed? You must be pleased that Wendy is back.'

Jack shrugged. 'Trying to keep myself decent, Liz. I've enrolled in beginners' Italian at Adult Ed. It struck me that I'm half-Italian and that maybe I should go over to Italy and see what I can find. Maybe I've got relatives. Must have. Anyway,' he said, looking at his watch, 'we'd better get back to the shop.' Liz patted his arm and said that learning Italian was a great idea.

CHAPTER 12

'YOU ARE LATE! *SEI IN RITARDO!*' admonished the teacher, tapping her watch and giving Jack a severe look. Jack hovered at the door, his ears glowing red, and stammered an apology. 'Well, don't just stand there. Come in and sit down!' she ordered. Jack slipped into the only vacant seat, only vaguely registering the attractive blonde woman sitting next to him as he ducked his head and tried to look small. He'd been held up talking with Duncan Snodgers about the Taroona place, but he could scarcely tell the teacher that. Besides, she had gone back to her lesson and seemed to have forgotten him, so he could study her closely without being rude. Ms Locatelli was a formidable woman with piercing blue eyes and dark hair pulled back into a severe bun. She spoke perfect English and explained that she had lived in Australia since she was a small child. Now she was asking if any of them had Italian connections. He put up his hand. His father came from Trieste.

'Hmm,' she said. 'I've never been there, but they say it's a beautiful city.' She seemed to have forgiven him for she gave him the ghost of a smile.

The woman sitting next to Jack had also put up her hand. He family were from Naples, she said. Ms Locatelli raised an eyebrow at that. At the end of the lesson, Jack tried to apologise for being late, but she waved him off brusquely. 'Just try to be on time next week,' she said imperiously as she swept out of the room. Jack felt like a small child again, sitting behind a school desk in Queenstown being admonished for not doing his homework.

The blonde student sitting next to him laughed. 'She's a bit of a sourpuss, isn't she?' Jack turned to her and smiled his agreement. She held out a slim hand for Jack to shake, 'I'm Fran Sorrentino. It's short for Francesca.' She had brown eyes and a steady gaze. They shook and her hand felt small and delicate in his paw. 'Anyway,' she sighed. 'I must be off to see to the kids. Nice to meet you, Jack.' She picked up her books and left, leaving a faint trace of perfume in her wake.

CHAPTER 13

'TA DA!' CHIRRUPED LIZ, waving an identikit picture about as she entered Jack's office. 'I know who Baldy is!' Jack's ears were pinned back. 'His name's Les Jetson,' she said with a triumphant smile. 'He used to live around the corner from mum and me at Goodwood.' She sat in the spare chair and proffered the drawing to Jack. 'Figjam!' she added.

'Eh?' Jack raised an eyebrow.

'Jeez you're an old dinosaur, Jack. It means, you know, "Fuck I'm Good Just Ask Me."'

'Yeah, right,' replied Jack, scrutinizing the mug the artist had drawn from the kids' description of Baldy. 'Ugly bugger. Dumb but mean.'

'You're not wrong, Jack. He's maybe five years older than me so I never had anything to do with him when I was a kid, but he stood out in the neighbourhood even back then, when he had hair.'

'Does he have form?' Jack asked.

Liz shook her head. 'Nah, he's "known to the police" as we say, but he never went to court. The last I heard, he'd gone to Melbourne, maybe five or six years ago. My prediction is that once we get hold of him and get some DNA, it'll all be over for him.'

Jetson had come to the attention of the Melbourne police too. Senior Sergeant Andrew Slater told Liz on the phone that Jetson was suspected of peddling drugs and pimping girls around St Kilda. 'He's work shy,' said Slater. 'Gives his occupation as "truck driver" but long hours behind the wheel don't suit him. He's "muscle" for brothel keepers and anti-union employers. Jetson's friendly with gangsters like Rocky Gangitano and the Munster but doesn't have the brains to start his own firm.

'Word is,' Slater continued, 'that he hung round the Hell's Angels until they decided he was bad news. Nobody would say what he did but it must have been pretty gross.'

'It all figures,' Liz said when she had related this to Jack. 'Jetson was a bully when he was a kid. The sort who stole kids' lunch money and broke into lockers. As far as I know, his parents still live out in Edinburgh Crescent.'

'Well, Liz,' said Jack, reaching for his coat, 'let's go and pay them a visit.'

Liz was pensive as they drove north out of the city centre along the Brooker Highway into Hobart's working-class suburbs. 'They were always nice people, Jack, so let's go easy on them. Christ knows what they ever did to deserve him.'

The Jetson house was one of many identical properties in the long, curving street that bisected the Goodwood Housing Commission estate, with its views of the zinc works in one direction and the Cadbury chocolate factory in the other. Strictly utilitarian, Goodwood boasted few trees despite the name. On race days, the residents could hear the callers and excited punters at the Elwick Racecourse nearby. Old 'Electric Eric' Reece, one time union organiser and former Labor state premier, still lived out here and Jack liked that about him.

'Here it is,' said Liz, pulling up beside a privet hedge with a manicured lawn. 'Takes me back, I can tell you.'

Mrs Jetson met them at the front door and invited them in. 'I'm Edna,' she said as she ushered them into the lounge. She was a middle-aged, matronly type, with a pair of glasses dangling down onto her imposing bosom, and a kind face. 'This is me better half, Charlie,' she said as she bustled through to the kitchen.

Jack's nostrils quivered at the promising smell of baking in the air.

Charlie Jetson looked up from where he had been working on his Tattslotto numbers and gave them a self-deprecatory shrug. 'I never win nothin',' he laughed, 'but hope springs eternal. Now, what can I do for yous?'

Liz was about to explain when Edna bustled in with a tray laden with tea and cakes. 'Iced these meself just this morning,' she said proudly. 'Best lamingtons in Tassie. Won first prize at the Hobart Show when I could still be bothered with that kind of thing. Apple pie's in the oven. If you'd come a bit later, you could have had some.'

Jack was disappointed about the pie but partial to a lamington: the Antipodean sponge cake whose origins Aussies and Kiwis disputed. His first bite told him these were indeed the work of a master. With the outsides well-soaked in the jam-and-cocoa coating and covered in moist coconut, and the sponge inside incredibly soft and light, Edna's were delicious. He scoffed one straight down and he didn't need much encouragement to take another, although Liz just nibbled at hers.

'Yairs, I remember you now,' said Edna, handing round more cake. 'You're Alice's daughter. Real tomboy you was if you don't mind me saying. Jeez, you've done alright for yourself. Detective Sergeant! Whoever would have guessed!'

Charlie coughed to get her attention. 'Ah well, Edna. I don't think this is a social visit.' He peered over his halfmoon glasses and invited the guests to continue.

'That's alright, Mr Jetson,' Jack said. 'No harm in a bit of a catch up.' He could see that they were decent people, and he was in no hurry to interrogate them. In Tasmania it was downright rude not to engage in a bit of social talk before getting down to business, and besides, he knew that you could often glean quite a bit from what might appear to be inconsequential chitchat.

Edna beamed at him. 'We don't often get visitors,' she confessed. 'We're homebodies really. Charlie was a wharfie until he retired a year or two back. He did his back in years back when they still unloaded ships by hand. He goes down to the pub with his old mates occasionally, but mostly we're here or at the shack up at Bradys Lake.' She paused. 'We had some good times up there when the kids were little. Andrea—that's our daughter—she's done well. She's a schoolteacher over in

Bellerive, and Les …' She tapered off here and looked at her husband for support.

'Thing is,' sighed Charlie, 'I guess you're here about Les. No other reason unless it's about me greyhound barkin' and upsetting the neighbours!'

Liz concurred that they wanted to ask about Les.

'Not much we can tell you, really,' said Charlie. 'We haven't seen hide nor hair of him since he went to Melbourne. Went off with that mate of his, Custard something or the other. Bad news, that one.' He paused. 'When was that, Edna? Five, maybe six years ago?' Edna nodded and he continued. 'We've never heard nothing from him, and although it doesn't sound too good when I say it, it's best that way.'

'You don't get on?' Jack prompted and reached for another lamington. One more wouldn't hurt.

Edna smiled her consent and took over from her husband. 'He was always a difficult child. Not like our Andrea. Les was always getting into trouble. He was a bully really, and when he got older, he fell in with a bad crowd. Never had what you'd call a proper job or nothing. I dunno where we went wrong. We're honest people, Mr Martin. Liz here will tell you that. We tried everything with him.'

'Tried tough love. Spoiled him when we could,' sighed Charlie.

'With love,' Edna interjected.

'Yeah,' said Charlie. 'I got him taken on down the wharf when we found he'd been nicking off from school. Didn't

stick at it, though. Stuck at nothing. That's all I can say really.'
Charlie spread his hands.

'So you haven't seen him around recently?' asked Liz. 'Never
heard anyone else mention they'd seen him back?'

The Jetsons shook their heads in unison. Charlie thought
for a while and asked, 'He's been around Hobart, then?' Liz
nodded and Charlie said sadly, 'I guess he's in a lot of trouble
for two detectives to come looking for him.'

'We would very much like to speak with him,' Jack agreed.
'I can't tell you why we want to see him, but yes, it is serious.'
He produced a copy of the identikit picture and passed it to
Charlie and Edna.

'Ooh,' sighed Edna. 'That certainly looks like Les.' She
winced and touched her own neatly permed brown hair. 'What
has he done to his hair? What will he do next?'

Shortly afterwards, Liz and Jack stood up and thanked
the Jetsons for their help and for the tea and cake. Jack left
his card and the couple promised that if they did see or hear
of their son, they would contact him immediately. They
looked old and vulnerable as they stood at the door to bid
the detectives goodbye. Neither Liz nor Jack spoke as they
drove back into the city.

CHAPTER 14

JAYMEE-LEE WINCHESTER, as she called herself professionally, had the unpleasant sensation that someone was watching her. It had been going on for more than a week and the feeling was stronger than ever. It was if eyes were boring into the back of her head, so she sighed with relief when she unlocked her front door and closed it behind her. She tossed her car keys onto the hall table and put the bags of groceries on the island bench in the kitchen. She stood by the window and peered through the curtains. There was nobody out in the street and it was silent except for a tin can rattling down the gutter in the wind off the river. She was imagining things. She was nice to her clients. No reason for any of them to wish her harm. There was the one, though, who gave her the creeps. Bloke in a denim jacket with a shaven head. Something cruel about him. Smelled bad too. She picked up the phone to call Uncle Ernie but put it back down again as the kettle came to the boil. She was having the night off. She'd put her feet up with a glass or two of wine, microwave the spaghetti and meatballs, and watch TV. She wasn't much of a cook. Nor much of a reader either, not like Uncle Ernie, who loved to read the *Australasian Post* and stuff like that. No use ringing him, she realised, because it was his cards night down at Cyril's place in the Glebe.

The microwave pinged and she bent to take the half-full bottle of chardonnay from the fridge. The people upstairs were clomping round again. Herd of bloody elephants. Dinner set out on the table, she went through to the bedroom to change into her trackie dacks and T-shirt. Too thin, she thought, viewing herself critically in the mirror after she'd taken off her skirt and blouse. Uncle Ernie reckoned the punters liked a girl with a bit of meat on her bones. Boobs weren't too bad, and she could still pass for twenty in the right light. A bit thin in the face but sort of pretty, with fine mousy hair and blue eyes. Bum needed fattening up a bit. A few more years and she'd get off the game and buy a milk bar, mixed business, something like that before she got too old to attract clients. Buggered if she wanted to go back into anything like Old Ma Ashford's house. She'd love to buy the Renown in North Hobart. Reminded her of when she was a kid and she'd buy lollies and drink Spiders there. Maybe get a husband? Nah. She'd been there done that. They were lazy, smelly creatures once they got their hooks into you. Thought they owned you. She liked the vicar well enough, but she was kidding herself if she imagined he'd marry her even though he reckoned he loved her. She laughed as she pulled on her dacks—the ones with a thick white seam and studs down the outside—'Easy Access Strides', an old boyfriend had called them. Now there was a pair, she giggled, the vicar and the hooker—wonder what the bishop would make of that!

Some faint change in the air made Jaymee-Lee pause with the fork halfway to her mouth. She placed the fork down as quietly as she could and stood up slowly, with her head tilted, almost sniffing the air. There it was, a noise coming from the spare bedroom out the back, the one facing into the hillside! The floorboards creaked. She cleared her throat and called out 'Who's there?' Her voice sounded weak and quavery, so she tried again, more firmly this time, and pulled the sharpest knife from the block standing on the bench. There was no answer, so summoning all her courage, she flung open the door leading to the central corridor and crept along it slowly, holding the knife before her. She screamed when she saw the figure standing motionless in the faint glow from the streetlights. He was big and he had a horrible face like a demon or something out of your worst nightmares. Jesus, he was coming towards her! She screamed again and turned to run. She wasn't quick enough. The demon grabbed her from behind, clamped a big hand over her mouth and twisted the knife from her grip.

'Don't scream again,' the demon growled. 'One more time and you're dead, so you are.' He had an accent, and she could swear she'd heard the voice before. He tied something around her face, forcing the cloth into her mouth, and then forced her hands together and bound them tightly. He prodded her to move back into the kitchen, forced her down onto a chair and pulled the blind down, acting with lightning speed. She almost wet herself at the sight of him. He was wearing a rubber mask, she realised, like one of those they sold in shops around the time of Halloween. At least he was human, well sort of.

'Well, well, ye wee hoor,' he snarled. 'I seen your card in the public telephone boxes: "Jaymee-Lee Winchester … Petite … Curvy … Call Me." ' He snorted derisively. 'Viv-vivacious, too!' He was reading one of the cards Uncle Ernie had had printed for her. 'Well, Jaymee-Lee Winchester—or should I call ye Val Dark?—I have a wee bone to pick with you.'

Irish. That was it, she realised. His accent was Irish. How did he know her real name?

'Don't hurt me, mister,' she pleaded, the cloth muffling her voice.

'What's that, ye little hoor?'

'Don't hurt me, mister. I'll do what you want. You can fuck me, anything. I've got money too.'

He laughed mirthlessly. 'There's nothin' ye've got that I want. Now, we're going for a drive in my car, so before we go, I'll have to put this wee bag down over your head, so I will.' He pulled a flour bag down over her head, secured it with a drawstring, and pushed her roughly in the back. 'Come on, let's have ye, ye little hoor.'

A blast of cold air rushed to greet her as he opened the front door and prodded her down the path, seizing her elbow impatiently when she stumbled over the step halfway down. She had started to cry, but he took no notice. She heard a car door creak open, and he thrust her inside and slammed it shut. He cursed when the car failed to start, and she found herself hoping that it wouldn't go, and he'd tell her to get back inside. She'd not say anything to anyone if he let her go, she promised, but he ignored her. The car started with a roar and her hopes died. He went through the gears and she could feel that they were driving downhill. She began whimpering but he told her roughly to shut her yap or he'd deal with her so he would. She tried to recall the turnings in the streets but after a while she gave up and just sat there, shit-scared about what he planned to do with her. A match flared and she smelled tobacco smoke. She'd given up six months earlier and the craving came back. The man said nothing more for a while but then he started muttering to himself and she heard him flipping through the pages of a book. A street directory, she realised. He was looking for somewhere. The car twisted and turned along what must have been a minor road for maybe an hour, until finally the man slowed and brought the vehicle to a halt. O Jesus, was this where he was planning to kill her? She started to cry again, big sobs this time, that made her gag on the cloth pressing into her mouth.

'Out, ye little hoor!' he shouted as he opened the passenger side door and when she refused to move, he grabbed her by the arm and yanked her out roughly. 'Ye'll do as I say if ye know what's good fer ye!'

She complied meekly and he shoved her ahead of him down what seemed to be a rough path, prodding her in the back and swearing all the time. A door creaked open and warm air hit her in the face. Once inside, he cut the cable ties from her wrists with a sharp knife, pulled the flour bag up from her head, and removed the gag. He was still wearing the mask—or perhaps had put it back on. 'Now, ye wee hoor,' he snapped. 'Get in there and do your business because it's going to be a long night.' He propelled her into the lavatory and sat in a kitchen chair nearby. 'Ye can't escape, if that's what ye're thinking.'

She was bursting, so she complied gratefully. When she came back into the room, walking stiffly from the constrained position in the car, she looked around her. It seemed to be a rural cabin. There must be electricity because the lights were on. There were no curtains on the windows, but it was too dark outside to see anything.

'Now, lassie,' he growled. 'I'm lockin' ye in the back room. There's a wee bucket for your business if ye need it. No windows, so there's no way out unless I want there to be. Have ye got that?'

She nodded and the tears started again. 'Why are you doing this to me?' she sniffed. 'I've done nothing to you mister.'

His laugh was brutal. 'Ye'd be too ignorant to know this, but in India, when they want to catch a tiger, they tether a wee goat to a post on the edge of the jungle as bait. Ye're the fuckin' goat, so ye are. Now, get in there and lie down and I don't want to hear the slightest peep out of you.'

Jaymee-Lee Winchester obeyed. It was a windowless storeroom or walk-in pantry. She sat on the thin mattress on the floor with her head in her hands and wept, searching in her mind to remember the prayers the nuns had taught her.

CHAPTER 15

CUSTARD SPROULE DROVE CAREFULLY as per Mr Sokolov's orders, suppressing the urge to do wheelies and doughnuts like he'd always done when there were no coppers about. 'Don't attract attention,' Sokolov had warned. 'We don't want police sniffing round.' Custard pulled up at the side gate of the old Derwent Park factory, got out, and pressed the buzzer, though he knew that Sokolov would be watching through the surveillance camera and liked to make him wait. He stamped his feet against the cold and shivered in his thin cotton jumper. Nobody lived around there. The plant was in the middle of an old industrial area across the railway lines from the local shopping centre. It was far from the touristy areas of Hobart. Eventually the gate opened, and Custard went through the factory doors. Sokolov was economical with words, his natural taciturnity coupled with a poor command of English. He jerked his head to indicate that Custard should follow him up the stairway to the office. This part of the building was much as it was when steel fabrication had ceased. A yellow overhead crane sat on rails thirty feet above the concrete floor and steel beams were stacked along the back wall. A big box girder still sat on steel trestles where welders had left it when a clerk brought their redundancy notices. The front part of the premises, Custard knew, had been converted into a brothel, and was separated from the factory by a locked door. In one of his rare attempts at humour, Sokolov had muttered that the new business was more profitable than steel fabrication and was immune to the business cycle—although he didn't phrase it so elegantly.

Sokolov's office was spartan: a cheap desk and chairs, a calendar with Miss June showing her charms on the wall, and a view through a filthy window over the nearby concrete batching plant. A safe stood in the corner. The drugs storeroom was next door. Maybe Sokolov wanted him to step up sales round the schools or something, Custard thought. They'd put the fear of death into the old firm's dealers, the Mitropoulos lot. Fuckin' wusses. Sokolov had a rifle and ammo in a cupboard. One of them Russian Kalamazoo things. Custard had seen him cleaning it. At the same time, he'd started asking questions about that copper, Gordon Paisley, who was doing a stretch over in the Pink Palace. Mixed up with the Mitropoulos lot. Something was up, but Sokolov didn't tell you nothing. Sokolov could hardly shoot Paisley in his cell, but he was planning something.

A man Custard hadn't seen before, wearing an immaculate pinstripe suit and red tie, was sitting behind the desk. Sokolov made no move to introduce him, and the Suit said nothing, languidly smoothing the wrinkles from his sleeve and watching Custard through silver-rimmed glasses. 'Sit,' Sokolov ordered, pointing to a chair in the middle of the room.

Custard sat and almost dared to open his mouth to ask what was going on but thought better of it. Sokolov's face was as impassive as ever. He suddenly slapped Custard sharply on the right ear. It hurt, but Custard kept quiet. Sokolov boxed the other ear harder, and it hurt even more.

'Jesus, Mr Sokolov,' Custard whimpered. 'Wozzat for?'

'Shut up,' Sokolov hissed. 'We ask questions. You answer. You know why you here.' He bent down and prodded Custard in the side of the neck and Custard screamed: the pain was unbearable, some sort of pressure point. 'I say again,' Sokolov prompted. 'You know why you here, Custard.'

'Please, no! Honest Mr Sokolov, I done nothin'.'

'You are liar, I think,' Sokolov snorted. 'You would like that I hurt you neck again?'

Custard shook his head, casting the Suit a terrified look. 'You gotta make 'im believe, mister,' he pleaded. 'I ain't done nothin'.' The Suit stayed silent, studying Custard with cold blue eyes magnified by his glasses.

'OK, Custard, my friend,' said Sokolov, patting Custard on the cheek with feigned affection, his steel teeth bared in a false smile. 'I tell you why you here. Police raid the house in Taroona, and we not happy.'

'I done—' Custard started to say, but Sokolov put a finger to his thin, cruel lips.

'Now, I think you know how cops know and you will tell me, yes?'

'Please,' Custard begged, but Sokolov wasn't listening. He

pulled Custard to his feet by the jumper and pushed him towards the door.

'You go down to factory floor, Custard, and I follow.'

Custard obeyed, hoping that the interrogation was over, and he would be allowed to leave. There was a sheila he had his eye on at one of the schools nearby where he sold drugs, he remembered. Sokolov, however, motioned that he should lie down face first on the concrete floor, among the patches of oil and rat shit. Custard did so, shivering from fear and cold. There was a jingling sound. He craned his neck and saw that Sokolov was bending down with a chain lifting sling.

'Now, Custard,' laughed Sokolov, 'I give you bit of a lift and you go flying.'

He wound the sling round Custard's ankles, reeved it by passing one ring through the other, dropped the ring on the hook and pressed the 'up' button on the overhead crane's control pendant. Custard was hoisted fast feet-first towards the underside of the crane. When he was dangling twenty feet above the ground, Sokolov let go of the 'up' button and pressed 'travel' and walked along as the crane bore Custard 'north' towards the end of the building. Custard screamed when the crane crashed into the end of the runway and the impetus swung him into the corrugated iron wall, narrowly missing a steel building column.

'You scream loud, Custard,' Sokolov jeered. 'Nobody hear you. Now we go for coffee and maybe fuck the girls while you think why you up there.'

The Suit had descended the stairs and was looking up at Custard with his teeth bared in a vicious grin. Sokolov let go of the crane pendant and the two men walked to the end of the factory and went through the door into the brothel.

Custard's tears were running through his hair. The chain links were biting into his ankles. The pain was excruciating, but he was terrified his ankles would slip through the sling. The floor was a long way down. He rotated slowly. Time passed and the rotations ceased. His legs were numb, and his head was aching. How long would they leave him here? Nobody but Sokolov and the Suit bloke knew he was hanging up there.

It seemed like forever before Sokolov returned alone and called up to Custard. 'I bring you down now. You tell truth, Custard and all forgiven.' He lowered Custard rapidly onto the floor and loosened the sling. 'You stand up now and tell me everything, I think.'

Custard felt faint. The blood had run to his head. He had pissed himself and when he went to stand his legs gave way. 'Poor Custard,' mocked Sokolov. 'I think you learn lesson. Yes?'

'I'm sorry, Mr Sokolov,' Custard snivelled, looking up from the floor. 'I should have said that Les had Maxine at the Taroona place.'

'That better,' Sokolov cooed. 'Now you are cooking with the gas. Les had girlfriend there, so I think maybe at the other house too?'

'Maybe he did Mr Sokolov, but I dunno for sure.'

'I am very disappoint with you, Custard. I give you good

job, so why you repay me this way?' He shook his head in a simulacrum of sadness and gave a predatory grin. He changed tack and patted Custard's cheek again. 'OK, Custard. I believe you. Now we go pay Les a visit. He is naughty boy, I think.' He pulled on the black gloves he habitually wore, and they went out into the back laneway where the car was parked. 'Now, you drive us very careful, yes?'

CHAPTER 16

JACK MARTIN AND DUNCAN SNODGERS were standing on the edge of the pit, sharing a big black umbrella. Their faces were as mournful as the day. The earth had been piled up under the fruit trees and it was turning to mud in the rain. Mist hung over the hills and seagulls cried out on the grey waters of the Derwent estuary. Duncan's assistants were fussing about, packing up their equipment.

'It's a bad business, Jack,' said Duncan. 'We've found a bairn's body. Just the one. I don't think there's any mair of 'em.' His shoulders slumped.

Jack didn't look too closely at the little bundle. Duncan lit up a cigarette and Jack took one before he remembered that he'd given up. Sod it, he thought, cupping his hands around the flame of Duncan's lighter, and sucking down the smoke greedily. Jack said a silent prayer and the two men trudged back into the shelter of the garage. The rain was torrential now and he could smell snow in the air. There were fingerprints and other clues all over the house, Duncan advised. Most of them—apart from those of the children down in the cellar— were from three individuals. Jack was pretty sure they'd get a match with those of Les Jetson, for although the man the kids knew as Baldy had never been convicted of anything, he had been arrested a number of times and they had kept his prints on file. Jetson must have had associates, and they would have to check them all out. He was too dumb to have organised all this himself, Jack thought. A car squealed to a halt and they saw Simon Calvert's shock of red hair emerge. The pathologist trotted up the drive in the rain, juggling his doctor's bag and pulling on a blue waterproof jacket. He joined them in the garage and extracted his packet of Drum tobacco and papers from a pocket.

'G'day, men,' he joked. 'You couldn't choose a better day for it.' They didn't bother to reply and after he had rolled his smoke and taken a few puffs he nipped it out, pulled up the hood of his jacket and descended the ladder into the pit.

Ten minutes later, his red head emerged from the pit and he scurried over to the garage, kicking clods of mud off his boots on the way. 'Fuck,' he muttered, accepting one of Duncan's cigarettes, evidently forgetting the butt in his pocket. 'If I weren't a fucking atheist I'd pray.' He lit up and continued, puffing like a dragon as he spoke. 'It's a girl. As far as I can see in these conditions, there are no indications that she was killed.'

'So,' asked Jack, 'natural causes?'

'Well going on her age, which I put at thirteen, it's a bit early for that,' the pathologist replied. 'My guess—and don't quote me—is that she died of an illness. But all in good time, gentlemen.' He packed up his bag and signalled to his assistants that they should take the body away.

Half an hour later, Jack was sitting in his office in his squelchy shoes, watching the rain course down the window-pane. What a shit day, he thought. Why did he do this job? Why did he stop being an electrician and become a copper? What kind of bastard could let the girl die and shovel her body into a hole like a piece of garbage? He caught himself. If he brooded like this, he'd slip into a depression, he realised. He would have to buck up—see Dr Ziegler—and get on with it. He couldn't stop bastards like this, but he could find them and make them face punishment for their crimes. He had no illusions about the police force. He was still disgusted with it for persecuting gay people, and he hated the way they always sided with the rich and powerful. What was it that Simon Calvert had half-jokingly called the cops? 'The attack dogs of the bourgeoisie.' That was it, and Wendy would agree. Annabelle van der Merwe too. He was surrounded by lefties and was sounding like one himself. Eric Blundstone and his mates would go apeshit. Still, Calvert had quoted one of his revolutionary heroes as saying that a policeman's baton could be used both to direct traffic and beat up strikers. Jack liked to think that he played a socially necessary and useful role—and the thought of that poor kid in the hole made him certain of it. So, he admonished himself, less introspection and more action! His colleagues were combing the city looking for the culprits and Les Jetson's ugly mug was scowling out from the front page of *The Mercury*. They'd find the bastard and lock him up and throw away the key.

CHAPTER 17

LES JETSON KNEW HE WAS IN TROUBLE the moment Sokolov walked through the door, with Custard Sproule trailing sheepishly behind him. Sokolov looked at him with those dead eyes and shoved him down onto a kitchen chair. He was wearing leather gloves and a black leather coat that made him look like something out of the Gestapo. Les was scared of the steel teeth. Maybe he really did rip out throats with them? They didn't see Maxine peeping through the window. She had been about to walk round to the front door to see Les when she saw the car and had hidden behind the garden shed next to the tree ferns. Les had asked her to pop round and she agreed, and even though he was only ever after one thing, she would get some attention at least. She had met Sokolov once and wished she hadn't, but she was curious about what was going on.

'Why you lie to me, Les?' Sokolov demanded. 'You say you slut girlfriend never been to Taroona house. Don't lie again. Has she been here too?'

Les's Adam's apple wobbled, and his mouth was dry. 'I shoulda said, Mr Sokolov, that she was at Taroona, but she's never been 'ere.' He cringed before the man's stare and realised he was whining.

'You lie once. Why I believe she never come here?'

'I'm sorry, Mr. Sokolov, I never thought—'

'You never think Les. Now whole fuckin' business up shit river because you no keep dick in trousers. You no use to me now, except maybe you tell me where is Maxine.' He lit up one of his foreign cigarettes and blew the smoke in Les's face.

'Jeez, Mr. Sokolov,' Les babbled, ignoring the smoke. 'I looked after things real good for ya. Don't worry about Maxine, she's just a slut. She's got a place on Letitia Street. I'll make sure she don't talk. I'll do her if you want.'

'Pah!' said Sokolov, his voice devoid of anger or any other emotion. 'You kneel on floor, on tiles.' He beckoned Custard to come closer and produced a pistol, the barrel of which was elongated with a suppressor. 'Custard. You take gun. Shoot fucker.'

Custard stepped back, trembling. 'I can't do it, Mr Sokolov … It's murder.'

'You shoot or I shoot you. You choice, Custard.' He pointed to the back of Les's neck and proffered the gun, butt first. Custard's hand was shaking, but he took the gun and tried to level it at where Sokolov had indicated.

'Stop the shaking. Be a man,' Sokolov snapped. 'This one dangerous. I think he squeal. You want cops to get you?'

Despite the suppressor, the sound of the shot was loud in the little room. Les slumped face forward and bright red blood spurted onto the white tiles. Custard dropped the gun and fell to his knees, moaning. Sokolov showed no sign of emotion. He pulled Custard up by the collar and bared his awful teeth in a travesty of a smile. 'Good man,' he said. 'I own you now. You one of us.'

Maxine had ducked down below the windowsill and listened in increasing horror. She repressed the scream welling up in her throat. Surely to Christ they hadn't ... but a little voice inside her head said they had; they'd killed Les. If they saw her, she was dead. She crawled to the tree ferns on her hands and knees, dared one glance back, and slipped behind the garden shed. The back door was closed. They mustn't have seen her. Sweat was pouring down her face. Or was it tears? Maybe both. She ran through the gate that opened out onto the strip of common land that ran between the houses up to the bush. Safe behind a stand of wattle trees, she vomited and sank helplessly to her knees, her red curls falling over her face. They'd killed Les like the old dog her father had shot years ago. It was horrible, but Les had betrayed her. If it would have saved him, Les would have shot her just as Custard had shot him. These people were evil. Maybe even worse than Horse Whistle and them. She couldn't go back to her place in Letitia Street. She'd have to go back up to Falmouth, regardless of how bad her father was. She just had to get away. Didn't want to go to the coppers. Didn't trust 'em.

Meanwhile, Sokolov directed Custard to tear up a strip of carpet, urging him on when he faltered at the task. 'Now, wrap up body, Custard,' he ordered. 'Roll up and get bleach from car and clean floor. Good job, no?'

Custard obeyed. He had never been housetrained, but fear made him work feverishly and soon the floor tiles were sparkling. His face was white as the tiles.

'Now we put Les in boot of car.'

Les was heavy, a dead weight as the two men hefted his body in the length of carpet and placed it in the car boot.

'Now Custard,' Sokolov commanded. 'We go back in house and wipe all clean. Put cigarette butts in rubbish bag. Take anything that lead cops to us.' Sokolov was a demanding supervisor, and it was almost an hour later when the job was done to his satisfaction.

'What about the kids?' Custard ventured. 'One of 'em's sick.'

'Forget kids,' Sokolov shrugged. 'Too dangerous now. We get rid of Les and go back to factory. More kids come soon.'

They dumped the body, still rolled up in its shroud of beige carpet, in the bush near the Tolosa Street quarry and drove back to the factory, keeping strictly to the speed limit. Meanwhile, Maxine had thumbed a lift with a middle-aged truck driver and was headed up past Brighton on the Midlands Highway. To her surprise, the truckie shouted her a hamburger and chips from Mood Food and dropped her off at Conara without putting the hard word on her. She wondered if some girls had dads like him. He wished her a pleasant day, gave her a $20 note, and drove off with his load of machine parts and timber. There was a public telephone box near the junction, so she nipped inside and called 000, the emergency number, and asked for the police.

CHAPTER 18

BLUEY BISHOP POKED HIS GINGER HEAD around the door just as Jack was preparing to read through a stack of boring correspondence. A huge yellow zit was burgeoning on his forehead, but Jack ignored it.

'That sheila's been on the blower again, sir,' Bluey said. 'Same kind of thing as before, only this time it's about some place out in Glenorchy.'

Jack shoved the bumph to one side, leapt to his feet, and reached for his coat on the peg near the door. The two detectives hurried down the corridor to listen to the recording. *'You better get out there quick,'* said a young woman's voice. *'There's kids locked up and them blokes killed a man this arvo.'* Jack recognised the voice as Maxine Fowler's. She was sobbing as she hung up. The techies had already traced the call to a public phone box in Conara, 150 kilometres north of Hobart on the Midlands Highway. They'd work that one out after they had rescued the kids, Jack thought, but the chances were she was heading back to Falmouth.

Once again, the cavalry charged off from the cop shop— Jack and Bluey in one car with a carload of uniformed officers following with sirens wailing and lights flashing, blasting their horns at drivers slow to get out of the way. This time they didn't bother to knock on the door of the white weatherboard house with tree ferns down the side but smashed the door in and piled inside. None of the upstairs rooms were occupied. There was a strong smell of bleach in the kitchen. Some stairs led down to a locked door and they smashed this in too. Seven terrified kids were huddled together and shortly afterwards a social worker arrived and took them away to safety. Jack reckoned they were Asian kids, Thai or Cambodian perhaps, and they were a mix of boys and girls in the same age range as at Taroona. One of them was ill, with stomach cramps and a high fever, so they made an urgent call to the duty doctor.

Duncan Snodgers and his team arrived, donned sterile gear, and turfed everyone out of the house. 'The lassie said a man was murdered here, Jack?' Duncan queried, sniffing the bleach in the air. 'Looks like the place has been wiped clean, but we'll detect any blood traces with luminol. Chances are they did the deed on the kitchen tiles. Easy to clean.'

Jack left Duncan's team to their work and drove back to the station. Late in the day or not, he convened a meeting to brief the team about the new development. Firstly, he was pleased to report that seven more kids had been rescued. One had been taken to hospital and although he wasn't a doctor, it looked serious. When they were ready, they'd talk to the kids via an interpreter and get them to describe those who had imprisoned them so that an artist could make up identikit pictures. As for Maxine Fowler, Jack telephoned the local plod in Falmouth to keep a lookout for her.

He had just hung up the phone when Simon Calvert rang. 'Got a minute, Jack?' the pathologist asked and continued without waiting for an answer. 'That girl in the garden. She wasn't murdered. She had a ruptured appendix, and it was left untreated, so perhaps that's the same as murder. She was also in the first stages of pregnancy. My report's on its way … And Jack, I hope that you catch these bastards very soon.'

Jack sat for a while to digest what Calvert had said, then turned to his computer to check his email. He stared at the screen for some time before he realised he'd been reading the same sentence over and over without taking in its meaning. Not that it meant much anyway in the scheme of things. How was it possible for those men—it had to be men, it was almost always fucking men—to get these kids all the way from the Balkans or Cambodia or wherever to an innocent-looking suburban house in Tasmania, lock them up and abuse them? On all that long journey, through docks, through airports, across borders, not one authority had saved those kids, and it took a powerless young woman who'd struggled all her young life to make it stop. Jack sat with his head in his hands. For fuck's sake, he raged, that kid had died pregnant and in agony from a burst appendix and he hadn't been able to save her. He shook his head and realised that he was patting his pockets for a cigarette. It wouldn't do. He had to maintain a distance for his own sanity. He swilled the remnants of his lukewarm tea, closed down the computer, and went home—or what passed for it these days. He'd almost forgotten that he and Wendy were staying in Holmes's granny flat.

There was a wonderful smell wafting from the kitchenette when he arrived. Wendy gave him a peck on the cheek and informed him that there was vegetarian moussaka and salad for dinner, and that she had opened a bottle of red wine to let it breathe. 'Friday night, Dad,' she said. 'You're to leave the job behind and put your feet up.'

He thanked her and did put his feet up. This was the life. He could close the door and leave the stresses of the job behind. He was lucky to have such a fine daughter. Eventually, he knew, she would find a nice man and would move out, but for the present, she was here, and he cherished the thought.

'Oh, Dad,' she called from the kitchen. 'I forgot to say. There's a couple of letters on the hall table for you.'

'Bills, probably,' he replied, but he stood up and went to check. They'd had the mail temporarily redirected from Darcy Street. One of the envelopes did indeed contain an electricity bill and there was some stuff from the bank. He stiffened when he scanned the last envelope, which was addressed in an unpleasantly familiar hand. He opened it carefully with his letter knife after feeling to see if there was anything thicker than a sheet of paper inside. His spirits sank when he read the message inside:

> LISTEN MARTIN YOU CUNT. I HAVE THE
> WEE HOOR VAL DARK WHO CALLS HER-
> SELF JAYMEE-LEE WUNCHESTR AND I
> WILL KILL HER UNLESS YOU DO A SWAP

FOR HER. I WILL PHONE YOU AND TELL
YOU WEAR TO COME. <u>YOU BETTER COME
ALLOAN</u> OR THE GIRL GETS IT SO SHE WILL.

Jack swore and stuffed the letter in his pocket. He didn't
want Wendy to see it. Val Dark. He remembered her. She
was on the game. She was the niece of one of his snouts, Ernie Dark, Hobart's last bodgie, known as Mr Drainpipes on
account of his tight jeans—he'd never been a plumber. Val
had supplied him with some useful information a while back
and once again there was a connection with the disgraced
Detective Sergeant Gordon Carson Paisley. Wendy called
brightly that dinner was served so he put on a smiling face
and went through to eat.

CHAPTER 19

SOKOLOV WAS IN CONFERENCE with the Suit and Trixie Ashford, who was wearing a pink bri-nylon trouser suit that crackled with static when she moved. The Suit grimaced as he took a sip of the drink Custard Sproule had handed him. It was a tepid light brown liquid with specks of white in it and bore little resemblance to either tea or coffee. Trixie had declined the offer of a drink, probably because she had tasted the muck before. She was getting old, but she had a powerful, mannish frame and Custard was afraid of her. She had tiny eyes of indeterminate colour under waves of permed blue-rinse hair. A while back, she had run an upmarket establishment in Davey Street, catering to the city's movers and shakers, but a well-planned police raid had put an end to that. Now, she was out in the boondocks; still had a few loyal customers from the old place, but the Derwent Park brothel was a comedown, and she was determined to work her way back up to be Hobart's premier madam once again. Every so often she called in a favour or two from some of the 'names' she had in her old Davey Street customer book.

Trixie was hectoring Sokolov in a Kiwi accent. 'I thought we could rely on you. Now there's a new betch due and no-where to put it.'

Sokolov was deferential to the one he privately called The Old Bat, but he was seething with cold rage inside. 'It's how you say, the best made plans of man and mouse go up shit creek without oars?' he shrugged.

'Not good enough, Mister Sokolov!' She turned to the Suit and told him, 'They are not staying in the brothel so you, Stephen, will have to come up with alternative premises. Pronto.'

The Suit spread his hands wide in a gesture of conciliation. 'Look Trixie,' he purred, slipping into the colloquial speech he imagined she preferred, 'we've all lost big time on our investments, but there's no use going crook at Ivan and me. He's has taken good care of the little … err problem and we've brought Custard's cousin on board to replace that … asset we had to dispose of. We're shifting a lot of product, too. Sidelined the old Mitropoulos firm and have streamlined the import side. We'll keep the new livestock consignment in the factory, here. I'll evict some tenants who haven't been paying the rent on a big place on Strickland Avenue and Sokolov can move them in shortly. Big place set back from the road. Hippies rented it for a commune. I'll have 'em out shortly. Bikies'll work a charm. Once the hippies see them come in through the doors they'll shit in their pants.'

Sokolov was nodding agreement, his reptilian eyes flicking between his colleagues. 'Custard now safe. He help get rid of scumbag.' He smiled, his steel teeth gleaming dully in the dirty light from the window.

'OK,' Trixie said, nodding her blue bonnet and giving him a sharklike smile of her own in return. 'But no more slup-ups, understood?'

Sokolov hastened to reassure her, and the Suit looked at his watch—a gold Cartier. 'Look, I think we've covered all bases, so can we wind this up? I need to get out to the airport. Alan Bull will be over at his property if you need him, but I'll be tied up with the new Docklands development.'

He stood, brushing invisible flecks of factory grit from his Savile Row suit. Sokolov opened the door and bellowed down to Custard, who was lurking down on the factory floor with another man, smoking and drinking beer. 'Get car,' he ordered. 'Take friend to airport.'

Custard handed the keys to his cousin, Sean Hurd, who had just joined the firm. He insisted that his name was pronounced 'Seen'. He could spell good, too, he claimed.

'You drive, Sean,' Custard ordered. 'Remember what Mr Sokolov said about the road rules. We don't want no cops sussing us out. Oh, and Sean, don't never cross 'im.' He mimed a knife cutting his throat. 'Seen an' not heard,' he advised, giggling at the only pun he'd ever made in his life. A kid had come out with it at school.

Sean grinned obligingly and went out the back when the Suit descended the stairs. Trixie walked a trifle arthritically through the factory to the door leading into the brothel.

'See ya round like a rissole Mrs A,' said Custard as the door was closing. The old bag had legs like fence posts, he thought, not that he'd dare say anything to her face. He was buttering her up so that he might get a freebie from the girls now and then. To his horror, she turned and came back, pinning him with her mean little eyes.

'Don't get clever with me, sonny,' she warned. 'You do as you're told and keep your trap shut.'

Custard gulped and made a grovelling apology, where-upon she stumped out of the factory like a pink Beefeater in drag. This job was hard, Jesus Christ it was, he thought, remembering how Les's head had exploded. Maybe pissing off to Sydney was an option? He'd be fucked if he just walked out and Sokolov saw him round Hobart. On the other hand, it was easy money. Not like that chicken factory he'd worked in when he got the exemption from school. The stink and the blood and guts was too much even though the old blokes reckoned you got used to it. Jesus, no way he could come at chook anymore even if it was Kentucky Fried.

Outside, the car started and drove off and except for faint mechanical clattering sounds from the concrete plant and some loose iron tapping on the roof it was quiet. Sokolov had put his powerful legs up on the top of the desk and was staring at the ceiling with expressionless eyes. Soon he was dozing and dreaming he was back in Afghanistan, firing a heavy machine gun from a helicopter gunship at fleeing tribesmen. He'd wanted to try poison gas, like Mussolini in Abyssinia and Saddam on the Kurds, but the commanders had ruled it out.

CHAPTER 20

THEY WERE EXPECTING THE TELEPHONE CALL, but the sudden insistent ringing startled the three of them. Commander Holmes nodded and Jack picked up the receiver. 'Hello,' he said, his voice neutral. 'Inspector Jack Martin speaking.' The conversation was being recorded and Holmes had put it on speakerphone.

'Givvus yer mobile number,' demanded the caller, his Irish accent stark over the phone. Jack obeyed and the man repeated it back to him. 'Right, Martin, ye cunt, ye. Drive up the Lyell Highway to Gretna. Pull over near the pub and wait for me to ring. Any funny business and the wee girl gets it, so she does. Do you understand?'

Jack said he understood, and what did he want, but the man hung up without answering.

They had agreed that going in mob handed would most likely end in disaster. The man was angry, armed, and dangerous. Being held hostage by some nutter was a frightening prospect for Jack but he feared the man would kill Val Dark, aka Jaymee-Lee Winchester, unless they complied with his wishes. Jack would drive out alone to Gretna and await further instructions as the kidnapper demanded. Liz Flakemore would follow twenty minutes later in an unmarked car. They would be in radio contact together and with headquarters.

The techies traced the man's call to near Hamilton in the middle Derwent Valley. Liz was a trained firearms officer and despite her elfin size and pretty face, she was a jujitsu black belt and keen hiker and climber. Jack would never take her on and many criminals had misjudged her to their peril. When they knew exactly where the man had the girl, Liz could use her bushcraft skills to get close. Heavily armed officers would be on hand as backup and to close off roads where necessary.

It was barely 7:30 am, but Jack and Liz were already kitted out in full Tasmanian winter hiking gear and Liz's backpack contained food and drink, night vision goggles, handcuffs, and spare ammunition for her pistol. Both were wearing bulletproof vests under their clothing. Heavy rain set in as Jack drove off from the police station towards the Brooker Highway, merging into the stream of traffic heading north and west out of the city. Barring traffic congestion and unforeseen hold ups, it would take him under an hour to get to the hamlet of Gretna to await further instructions from the Ulsterman.

The drive was uneventful and after New Norfolk, the Lyell Highway was virtually deserted where it snaked its way through bush and farmland up the Derwent Valley. On a clear day, Jack knew, it was starkly beautiful, with vistas of the Derwent rapids, hop kilns, poplar trees, and the rim of mountains to the west. But the rain had set in hard and was bouncing off the asphalt as he pulled in next to the Gretna Green Hotel and unscrewed his thermos for a coffee. Visibility was down to a hundred yards. Fifteen minutes went by. He flinched when there was a tap on his window, but it was only the local busybody, demanding to know what Jack was doing, and he scooted off quick smart when Jack produced his warrant card. Another ten minutes ticked slowly by, and Jack was beginning to think it was a wild goose chase when his mobile buzzed. Meanwhile, Liz had driven into the hamlet and parked further back. They gave no indication that they knew each other in case the kidnapper was watching.

The caller didn't bother with preliminaries. 'Drive straight ahead to the top of the wee hill before Hamilton,' he ordered. 'Turn right into Thousand Acre Lane and drive towards the Pelham forest. Remember, drive real slow.'

After relaying the information back to base, Jack set off, drove slowly for twenty minutes, and turned into the lane after almost missing it because of poor visibility in the rain. Thousand Acre Lane was narrow, bumpy, and unsealed. It snaked higher and higher into the hills, and Jack was hard pressed to do 30 kilometres an hour in the deluge. The road cut across scrubby pastureland before entering a forest. Cows loomed up out of the murk, indifferent to the rain, watching the car and chewing. Jack had just slowed down to take a right-angle bend when a black-clad figure stepped out into the road and pointed a semi-automatic rifle at the windscreen. It happened too suddenly for Jack to do anything but hit the brakes and come to an abrupt stop.

'Get out!' the figure ordered—the same Irish voice as on

the phone. He was wearing a sou'-wester and a long Drizab-one coat and reminded Jack of a wasp because of the striped black and yellow bandanna covering most of his face. Jack got out and the gunman waved the rifle towards a gum tree at the side of the road. 'Put yer hands up on the tree and spread yer legs!' he ordered. 'Don't try nothing because I know my way round guns.'

He patted Jack down and grunted as he felt the bulletproof vest. 'Get it off!' the gunman ordered, and Jack complied, feeling vulnerable as he stood half naked in the rain. When Jack had dressed himself, the gunman motioned for him to walk into a narrow four-wheel drive track leading off north-wards into the forest.

'Can I get my coat?' Jack pleaded. 'It's bloody well pouring down!'

The man's reply was a poke in the back with the barrel of his gun.

The track went up steeply and the downpour had turned it into a small creek, the water making the going treacherous underfoot. After a while, the gradient levelled off and the walking became easier, although the rain still poured down relentlessly, and Jack was soaked through. The man ignored his polite request to know how much further they had to go.

'Keep walkin',' he growled. 'I'll tell ye when we're there.'

The track steepened again, and Jack could hear the man's breath labouring, but he didn't allow Jack to relax his pace. The rain had turned to sleet. By this time Jack was worrying seriously about hypothermia. He was relieved to smell wood-smoke and guessed they must be nearing their destination. They rounded a bend, and the cabin was suddenly there in front of them—a single-storey affair of overlapping vertical hardwood boards painted in sump oil. The wind was blowing the smoke from the tin chimney away to what Jack reckoned must be the east, almost parallel to the ground. His teeth were chattering, and he was looking forward to warming himself at the fire inside the cabin. His captor flung the door open and pushed Jack inside with the gun. It was warm inside, and almost homely because of the oil lamp burning on the big table in the centre of the room. Jack noticed a big kitchen dresser full of crockery, fishing tackle, oily tools, and a partially dismantled chainsaw. Jack raised an eyebrow at the framed portrait of the Queen hanging over the fireplace, along with a hand-stitched tapestry of the Lord's Prayer. They were out of place, perhaps, in a Taswegian male's den.

'Sit down!' the man ordered. It sounded like 'set dine' in his thick accent. 'Over there, ye cunt, ye.'

Jack was happy to comply, and his clothes were soon steaming in the heat from the combustion stove. There was a rubber Halloween mask lying on the table and he wondered why it was there. There was no sign of kids who might like such stuff.

'Now, Inspector Martin, ye cunt,' snarled the man. 'Here's the deal. Ye put my wee cousin Gordon away and I want him freed. That an' half a million dollars and safe passage out of

Australia for the pair of us. The wee hoor will take a message when we get a deal. Any bullshit and I'll shoot yous both dead, so I will.'

He removed the bandanna and the hairs on Jack's neck stood up. It could have been ex-Sergeant Gordon Paisley standing there before him, Dennis Lillee moustache, pumpkin head and all. The gunman's mad brown currant eyes never blinked, and Jack realised that he was deadly serious about the idiotic deal even though the plan had zero chance of success. The bloke was insane. Best not to upset him, though, Jack knew. Don't directly challenge him. Keep him talking.

'Do you think they'll agree?' Jack asked, striving for a friendly tone, though he remembered his own persecution at the maniac's hands.

'They better,' replied the gunman, tapping the rifle barrel.

'What about the girl?' Jack asked. 'Where is she?'

Without answering, the man unbolted a door in the far wall of the cabin. 'Get your wee hoor's arse out so that the nice peeler can see ye,' he commanded.

Jack heard the young woman gasp. 'You!' she gulped. 'No, it can't be. You're in prison!' She sidled though the door, keeping her distance from the gunman, and stood trembling with fear, but grateful for the stove's warmth.

'Shut it,' snarled the gunman. 'You helped put him away.'

Jack remembered that the disgraced Sergeant Paisley had demanded freebies at Trixie Ashford's old brothel and that Val had been forced to service him. The sight of the boofhead's cousin standing there must have made her skin crawl. 'A head on him like a pox doctor's clerk,' he recalled her saying when they met with her Uncle Ernie in the 'snakepit' of an inner-city hotel. 'That thing mounted up on you took the biscuit!' The poor woman was a pathetic sight. She looked on the verge of a nervous collapse, eyes staring wide over a tremulous mouth. Her makeup had run, making her look like a sad clown. She bucked up a little when she saw Jack, but her whole body was still shaking, and she started to cry.

The gunman laughed nastily. 'This hoor here is the wee goat, Inspector. Now I have the tiger although ye look a bit more like an old grey tabby cat if ye ask me. The arse on ye's moth-eaten!'

'Are you going to let her go?' Jack asked, ignoring the insults. 'That was the deal, swapping her for me.'

The kidnapper sniggered. 'Just shut yer trap and listen. I have the demands written here,' he snarled, waving a scrap of paper. 'Jaymee-Lee Winchester here is going to walk out to the main road and get a lift. It might take a little while, but somebody will stop. She can deliver the wee note to the peeler at Hamilton. I'll put the note in a wee bag so that it doesn't get wet.'

Val was not happy about the prospect of walking in the forest in that foul weather. She was a city girl and had no clue where she was. It was bitterly cold outside, and she had no raincoat, only her thin cotton tracksuit and runners. The rain was falling in thick sheets and drumming on the tin roof, and a demonic wind was hurling itself at the trees. Jack's teeth had stopped chattering by this time, but he was pleased when the man ordered Val to make some tea before she left. Jack gave her a reassuring smile, although he wasn't certain that there was anything to encourage her about.

None of them knew it, but Ivan Sokolov had tuned into the police radio frequency and was cruising up the Lyell Highway with a Kalashnikov covered by his coat in the back seat of his car. His sources had informed him of the Irish gunman's presence, and he feared he was a hitman hired by Angelo Mitropoulos. Sokolov was determined to crush all resistance to his firm's takeover of the drugs trade. He heard nothing more, so he gave up and drove back to Hobart. He was confident of finding his prey sooner or later.

CHAPTER 21

CUSTARD CLOSED THE DOUBLE GATES behind the white van, and it slid to a halt beside what had been a sand-blasting shop when the premises were used for lawful industry. Neither Custard nor Sean had ever done an honest day's toil and they were not in the least curious about what the place had been. They weren't curious about anything, really; as Johnny Rotten put it, they were 'pretty vacant'. The rain was pockmarking the big puddles round the yard. Sokolov was watching from his office window, his expression inscrutable. Bugger wouldn't come out into the rain to help, Custard muttered to his cousin. The driver jumped out and jogged round to open the van's back doors, jerking his head for Sean and Custard to come over. He was a thin-faced, wiry individual dressed in skin-tight blue jeans, oilskin jacket and black beanie.

'You help,' he ordered in broken English. 'Girls fighting a bit.'

Sour air wafted from the van when he opened the doors. Six young girls were cowering in the back, the compartment sealed from the front by a steel panel. They refused to move and one of them, a dark-skinned girl of perhaps 14, was defiant. 'You bad!' she screamed, eyeing the three men with hatred.

'Get hose,' the driver ordered, and Custard rushed to comply. There was a firehose in the sand-blasting shop. Custard dragged it out, Sean opened the valve, and a powerful jet of water spurted out. The driver grinned and aimed the jet into the back of the van. 'Little shower!' he laughed nastily. 'You come out now girls, I think!'

The defiant girl came barrelling out first, dripping water, and flew at her tormentor. She was quick and agile and before he could back off, she had raked her nails down the side of his face, only just missing his eyes. The man screamed and punched her viciously in the face. '*Suka!*' he yelled, dabbing at his face with a filthy handkerchief. Sean and Custard were standing by, too afraid to intervene, but Sokolov had rushed out of the factory and was shoving the driver away from the van. He was in an unusually foul mood after driving back from some unspecified business.

'*Chertov* idiot!' he hissed. '*Ne povredi ikh!*'

Custard and Sean were not Russian scholars, but they got the man's drift. The driver was still dabbing at his injured face and Sokolov had seized the girl by the waist and was manhandling her towards the factory door. 'Bring others!' he shouted over his shoulder. 'Now! *Nemedlenno!*'

The five others came out quietly, shrinking away when the men grabbed hold of them. 'Easy now,' said Custard, a ghastly grin revealing rotten front teeth and pointed incisors. 'Nobody's gunna hurt ya!'

When the girls were locked inside the factory, Sokolov slapped the uninjured side of the driver's face, then turned and did the same to Sean and Custard. 'Fucking idiots!' he raved. '*Suki! Kisok!* Girls valuable. You no mark them faces. If anybody hit them, only me. You understand, *pridurki*?'

They nodded meekly and Sokolov, mollified, continued in a softer voice. 'Girls stay here until afternoon. Later we take them to new house. OK? Now, bring dry clothes from store number one. Quick.'

The girls were shivering together by the far wall of the factory and they willingly swapped their wet clothing for the dry stuff Custard brought. He ogled them as they undressed, but Sokolov ordered him off. 'These ones Cambodian,' he informed the men, rubbing his thumb and forefinger together. 'Cost a lot. Make sure we know where they are all time.'

They could hardly hear him speak, so great was the racket of the rain drumming on the tin roof. They had no clue what Cambodian meant. The girls could have come from Mars for all they knew or cared.

CHAPTER 22

LIZ WAS HUNKERED DOWN in a thicket of wattle trees, watching the cabin. She had found Jack's car abandoned by the roadside and guessed what had happened. She had followed the jeep track through the forest, getting lost on spur trails a couple of times, but had finally stumbled on the cottage. She had circled right around the clearing and discovered what she took to be the man's big black Transit van sitting in a laneway just off what her map told her was the Hollow Tree Road. It was still raining hard but her trusty Gore-Tex was keeping out the worst of the water and she was warm in her thermals. She had the SIG Sauer P226 pistol in one hand and a cheese sandwich in the other. She could see Jack sitting in an armchair near the fire and Val Dark standing at the table. It looked like Jack was tied to the chair with blue rope. The kidnapper was moving in and out of her vision, brandishing a semi-automatic rifle, raving on by the look of it. She couldn't believe it. It was either Gordon Paisley or a doppelganger. He was laying down the law about something and Jack was nodding agreement under duress. Val Dark looked lost. Liz had tried to phone Derek Holmes when she saw the shack, but there was no reception. She'd just have to wing it.

What the hell? The door had opened, and the gunman was

shooing the girl outside. Very strange. Val stood uncertainly for a minute or so until the man said something Liz couldn't catch, and the young woman set off reluctantly towards the road near where his car was parked. The grey fabric of Val's tracksuit top was soon blackened by the incessant rain. Christ, Liz would have to help her, or she would soon perish from hypothermia. Reluctantly Liz dropped her sandwich and circled round through the bush. Val shrieked and put her hand to her mouth as Liz emerged in front of her on the roadside.

'Police!' Liz hissed. 'Just keep walking.'

Val looked like she was about to give up and lie down to die, but Liz urged her to keep going and when they were a reasonable distance from the turn-off to the cabin, she took off her waterproof jacket and ordered Val to put it on. She demurred but Liz insisted. It fitted, so Liz would just have to make do with her fleecy top and bulletproof vest.

'Now,' Liz said. 'Here's a mobile phone. When you get reception, ring up this number'—here she gave Val her card—'and tell them where you are. I reckon you'll get reception out at the main road, which is maybe a twenty-minute walk from here. Maybe you'll get it sooner. Someone will come along and pick you up.'

The two women parted company, with Liz walking back towards the cottage.

Back inside, the gunman was eyeing Jack with distaste.

'You a fuckin' Taig?' he demanded.

Taig, Jack knew, was a derogatory term for Catholics used

by some Protestants in Northern Ireland. Jack shrugged. He was a lapsed Catholic, but he figured this lunatic wouldn't make the distinction. Probably thought Catholic and Protestant were fixed biological categories.

'I guess you are then,' said the man. 'A Taig that is.'

'You're Irish?' Jack asked to keep the man talking. He didn't realise that he had stepped onto a sectarian minefield.

'No, I am not fuckin' Irish!' the man shouted, saliva spraying from his mouth. 'I'm fuckin' British!'

'OK,' Jack soothed. 'I get the distinction. You're what they call an Ulster Loyalist.'

The man was calmer. 'Too right I am,' he agreed. 'Ulster is right, and Ulster will fight! I've done my bit for Northern Ireland'—it sounded like Norn Iron—'to stay British and make the Croppies lay down. They don't call me Mad Dog for nothin', so they don't.'

Jack let this pass. 'You haven't told me your name,' he prompted. 'Seeing as how we look like spending some time together, we should introduce each other.' It was a strain buttering up this creep, but he had to forget about the attacks and just do it.

'I know who you fuckin' are, mister,' Mad Dog snarled. 'Ye're the bastard who sent my cousin down, so ye are.' He stared at Jack and added in a softer tone, 'I grew up with Gordon on the Shankill Road. More like brothers than cousins, so we were.' His mercurial mood shifts were alarming.

'So, what's your plan?' Jack asked, sounding as reasonable

as he could. 'You must have it worked out where we go from here.'

'We wait until I say so,' Mad Dog replied, 'then we get in my van. When we get phone reception we can negotiate. Don't forget I have this.' He tapped the rifle and ran his hand lovingly down the barrel.

The rain had eased off just a little, for which Liz was thankful, but water was still dripping from the trees and she was sopping wet and cold. The man had got angry, and she had wriggled closer so that she could get a clear shot if necessary, but Jack seemed to have calmed him down and it looked like they were chatting amicably together. Liz hoped it would stay that way and slipped off silently through the trees to the Transit van. She took out her Swiss Army knife and punctured all four tyres. The escaping air made a satisfying hiss and the van slumped onto the gravel like it had been shot. She surveyed her handiwork gleefully, then circled back through the wet scrub to her hiding place.

CHAPTER 23

NORNRY HAD RUN TILL SHE WAS EXHAUSTED and was hiding behind a row of grey cement-block shops. For all that she knew, she was on a different planet. It was so cold even though the rain had stopped. An icy wind was blowing down off the big bald mountain and the light was beginning to fade. She feared that the bad men would be hunting for her. Maybe when it got dark it would be safe to go. The trouble was, she didn't know where to go to or what this place was. Nothing looked familiar and all the people she had seen were white. Nobody was walking. They were all in cars except for a boy who went past on a bicycle and shouted something at her. She was shivering. They had given her a cotton jumper after that horrible man had turned the hose on them, but it was too thin to keep her warm.

Nornry was hungry too, and even though she had drunk some water from a tap next to a factory wall she was still thirsty. There was a funny smell coming from one of the shops. Fat frying, she thought. There were coloured lights in the window spelling out something in the strange script she had seen sometimes in Battambang. She crept up to the front of the shops and saw there was a crate outside of another shop. It was full of bread like they had fed her on the boat and in the van, so she grabbed a loaf and ran off. Nobody saw her, so she slowed down. There was a big blue bin under a streetlight. She couldn't read what the sign said, but when she looked inside, she saw it was full of clothes. She could burrow inside the clothes and get warm and when she had to go, she could wear some of them. It wasn't stealing because maybe people didn't want the clothes anymore. She climbed up into the bin and soon she was much warmer. She was lucky, too, because the rain had started again. She went to sleep remembering how she had hit that horrible man on the back of the head with the spanner. She hoped it had hurt. She wouldn't care either if he was dead, although it was a sin to kill.

CHAPTER 24

SOKOLOV WAS FURIOUS. He kicked the prostrate Custard in the side and raged at him in two languages. He was a *pizda*. An idiot. A stupid asshole who would get them all killed. Custard did not respond, but he sat up groggily when Sokolov tipped a bucket of water on him. 'Where girls?' Sokolov demanded. Custard's head ached and he wanted to vomit, but he searched his feeble brain for an answer to why Sokolov was so angry. It came back. He'd been trying to have a bit of fun with one of the girls and she'd started screaming the place down. 'All right! All right!' he'd whined, backing off. Then it all went black. One of them must have got behind him and bashed him on the head. Christ, what had he done to deserve this? Hurt like fuck.

'Find girls!' Sokolov yelled, so Custard staggered over to the back doors of the factory and looked out. It was dark, but the rain had stopped. He could see a couple of them hiding in the shot-blasting shop. He'd round 'em up and get Sokolov off his back. Shit. He remembered what had happened to Les Jetson—what Sokolov had made him do to Jetson—so he started grabbing the girls and shoving them back inside the factory. Another pair were hiding up in the cab of the over-head yard crane. After he climbed up the ladder and mimed throwing them down, they descended quickly enough. That left two, maybe he'd be spared another bollocking, or worse. It started to rain again, and he wished he wasn't there. Bloody tarts. Why did they have to make things so fuckin' difficult? 'Aha! Gotcha!' he jeered, pulling another one out from behind some rusting girders. Only one to go. Jesus, it was that hellcat. He didn't know if he was more scared of her or Sokolov. It would have been her that cracked him one. Christ, he was feeling woozy again and he could feel blood seeping out into his hair. 'Come out, ya little slut!' he bawled, but it was dawning on him that she'd escaped. Fuck. He was for it now!

Sokolov had simmered down. His eyes were back to their normal glacial hue; dead, no life in them. 'We must find girl,' he said, his voice toneless. 'Ring Sean. I get driver back and we search until we find her.' Custard didn't like the way Sokolov was looking at him. When Sean and the driver arrived, Sokolov produced a map and divided the area into quadrants. They would take one car each and search until they found her. Custard hoped they did, for his own sake.

CHAPTER 25

MEANWHILE, A FEW KILOMETRES AWAY, out near the Tolosa Street quarry, apprentice wood-butcher Terry Adams and his new girlfriend Janice Myers were all over each other in the back of his Sandman panel van. The van was his pride and joy. It had decals of palm trees and flames and everything that made it the coolest bus in Glenorchy. He'd bought it for $300 from a bloke whose wife reckoned he was too old for it. The bloke had winked and told Terry he'd gone round in it for a while with a cop's daughter. Reckoned the cop had gone ballistic when he saw her in it! Terry told him he'd look after it. True to his word he'd polished it every weekend till it shone like new, though it was getting on a bit. Janice loved it. He wasn't sure if she was 17, but jeez she was a goer! Didn't seem to mind his zits. Still had her Claremont High School uniform on. Or rather half on. She thought the inside with the carpet and big speakers was the ticket. Even had a cabinet with top shelf drinks in it. Fair dinkum, you wouldn't read about it, she was gettin' real hot just when he needed to do a piss! Gawd, he'd got her bra off and everything. She was steamin'! 'Don't be too long,' she purred, and he knew he was on a promise.

The rain had stopped, and the clouds had lifted a bit as

he unzipped his strides and started to piss, raring to get back. What's that? he wondered. Something white coloured in the bushes. He parted the bushes for a better look. You sometimes found stuff people had thrown out and you could get a few bob for out here. Oh, good Christ, no! It couldn't be—but it was! A body was lying there staring at the night sky, or part of it was because it was sticking out of a carpet or something. No way it was a tailor's dummy. He'd never seen a dead body before, but he was sure he had now.

Terry scrambled back to the car and said Jesus no! when Janice wanted to go back where they'd left off. He was babbling incoherently as he started the car and backed out towards the road, with Janice staring at him as if he'd gone mad. There was a public phone box down the road a bit. He jumped out of the car and made the 000 call with shaking hands.

'Yeah, that's right,' he squeaked. 'A body at the Tolosa Street quarry. Dead ... Yeah. Fuckin' dead I'm telling you.' He refused to give his name and hung up. Terry dropped Janice off at home and reversed the Sandman into his parents' driveway. Near hit the fencepost his hands were shaking so much. Almost cried at the thought of it. The old man would've gone crook too.

'Keep it zipped,' he'd warned Janice, running a forefinger across his mouth. 'We don't want to get mixed up with no coppers. We ain't seen nothing.' He hoped she wasn't too pissed off with him.

He was still shaking when he lit a cigarette and turned on

the stereo in his bedroom. Nirvana. 'Smells Like Teen Spirit'. Jeez, he loved that song. The olds were watching television and had only grunted when he'd come in. Sky could fall in and they wouldn't see nothin' when they was watchin' a western.

Back at Derwent Park, Sokolov had decided to call it a day. He and his employees were standing outside Julia's fish & chip shop and he'd allowed them to get a feed. Pah, fish & chips. He'd kill for a bowl of borscht. He'd figure out what to do with Custard and the other cretinous fuckwit, but for the moment he needed them. They'd start again at first light, although he would patrol about from time to time before it was time for bed. Sleep in the office or at Trixie's brothel.

Sokolov went to bed early that night and woke up bathed in sweat when the dream came back. His best friend Kolya was sprawled there in the bazaar with his innards spooled out like a squid's tentacles, the smoke from the rocket still hanging between the ruined buildings. The authorities had put them straight in the army from the orphanage. It had never occurred to either of them to question their right to do so, but Sokolov was a survivor. He'd survive now. Claw out a place in the world whatever it took. No way he was going to let a little tart get the better of him, he swore.

Twenty yards away, Nornry was fast asleep in the Salvos' old clothes collection bin. Sokolov had peered inside but failed to see Nornry's slight form hidden among the old clothes.

CHAPTER 26

LIZ HAD NEVER FELT WETTER OR COLDER as she crouched down watching the shack, not even when she had been caught in a blizzard up near Cradle Mountain. Something would have to happen soon, or she feared she would die of exposure. It was sleeting and the sky was full of blue-grey altostratus clouds threatening a big dump of snow. Maybe she had been hasty in giving Val her coat. Chances were the lucky woman was warming up with hot food in front of a roaring fire! Still, Jack's life was in danger and she had to stay. If only she could get a signal on her phone and get someone to relieve her.

Hello! Action! The gunman was opening the door. He'd been poking round in the combustion stove, so she figured he was coming to get more wood. His bulky form blocked her view of Jack in the interior. She pulled out her pistol and moved quickly and silently, praying that she wouldn't snap a twig or do anything else to attract the man's attention. He was standing up with an armful of wood when Liz sneaked up and shoved the barrel of her pistol between his shoulder blades. She could see blackheads and whorls of ageing skin on the back of his neck.

'One move and you're dead!' she hissed. 'You're under

arrest. Now, drop the wood and get down on your knees.'

The man complied. Liz closed a handcuff around his wrist and snapped the other cuff round a solid looking half-inch water pipe leading from a rain tank. The click was an intensely satisfying sound. She frisked him and pulled a pistol from one coat pocket and a knife from the other. She was moving past him cautiously when he swung one of the logs at her, shouting that she was a wee bitch, so she was. In answer, she booted him onto his side, and he lay there cursing in the slush, with his arm hanging off the pipe. Inside, she sawed through Jack's bonds and he stood up flexing his fingers to restore the circulation. Liz patted him on the shoulder and passed him the rifle.

'Keep hold of this,' she ordered. She wasn't taking any chances with the lunatic outside. 'Now. I'm half frozen and dying for a cup of tea.' Jack lit the gas stove under the kettle while Liz gratefully warmed her bum at the fire and went to check on the gunman and bring him inside.

The water pipe had been wrenched out of the tank. The gunman had pulled the handcuffs free and disappeared.

'Quick!' yelled Liz, running into the driveway. 'The bastard's probably headed for his car.'

If so, she knew he wouldn't get far.

The black van was still sitting forlornly on its four slashed tyres, but there was no sign of Mad Dog. He had vanished, although whether along the road or into the bush they couldn't tell. Just then, they heard an approaching engine and a police four-wheel drive vehicle roared up. Jack got the driver to radio through the information that Mad Dog had escaped and was on the loose somewhere in the forest. All units should break cover and search. He wasn't believed to be armed, but he was still dangerous.

A couple of hours or so later, after retrieving Jack's car and vest from Thousand Acre Lane, Liz and Jack were steaming over a radiator back in the Hobart cop shop, drinking hot coffee and munching on croissants. Someone had produced some old clothes and Liz was grateful, although she was flopping about inside them, joking they would fit an elephant. Val Dark had made a statement and had been taken to her Uncle Ernie's house. Traumatised but otherwise unscathed by her ordeal, she refused to go back to her flat, convinced that the gunman might return.

Mad Dog had left his passport and a return airline ticket to Manchester at the shack, and these identified him as William Craig Bloat, 56 years old, domiciled on the staunchly Loyalist Shankill Road in Belfast. Commander Holmes was expecting more information about him from the Royal Ulster Constabulary. Wintry night had fallen, and the search of the Pelham forest had been suspended until first light. It looked like Mad Dog was in for an Arctic night. Holmes agreed that the report on Jack's desk about the cadaver at the Tolosa Street quarry could wait until the morning. Five minutes later, they had packed up and were on their way home through the rush-hour streets full of cars and scurrying pedestrians anxious to get out of the incessant rain.

CHAPTER 27

NORNRY HAD NO IDEA WHERE SHE WAS, but she was a plucky girl. It was pitch black. She was in a big steel bin. The air was freezing cold, but it was warm where she was lying among the old clothes. She drifted off into a pleasant reverie. Maybe it would be time for the rice harvest in her tiny village between Battambang and the Thai border. Her parents told her of the terrible times under Pol Pot, but things had got better. There was enough to eat and the men in black no longer ruled over them. Sometimes Vietnamese soldiers with red stars on their pith helmets had come but they had left the villagers alone. There had been fighting and her father told her that the Khmers Rouges sometimes came over the border. The thought of her village stabbed her heart and she was suddenly fully awake. Men had come in the night, she recalled. Not soldiers, but they had guns and they shot Mr Vang the headman when he argued with them. She didn't know if he was still alive, but she often prayed for him. She had clung desperately to her mother, but a man had hit her with his rifle, and they tied her hands together and threw her up on a truck. Bopha, Chandra, Mey and Rith were there with some boys and girls she didn't know. The truck drove off and she could still hear her mother screaming.

The sun came up. They were thirsty, but the truck did not stop. She knew from the position of the sun that they were going west. There was a man with a gun in the truck tray and when they came to a town, he threw a big tarpaulin over them, but she could see under the edge that the script on the shopfronts meant they had crossed the border into Thailand. When the sun was high in the sky, the truck stopped, and they were allowed to do their business. The men gave them some rice and water and screamed at them to get back up. She didn't have her red-checked Khmer headscarf, the *kramah*, and she worried about sunstroke. The next time the truck stopped it was dark. They were allowed down again, with the men standing round pointing their guns to make sure no one tried to escape. Then they drove on and on through the night and she slept, sometimes waking up sobbing.

She woke when the truck stopped, and she could hear bad men shouting in Thai. The truck was parked next to a jetty where there were fishing boats tied up. The men came back and started yelling at them again to get down. Then they tied their hands together and put another rope through their legs, so they had to move together like a snake. They didn't want to go aboard the big boat, but the men cursed and hit them and drove them up the gangplank with their rifle butts. She tried to look them in the face to make them see what they were doing was wrong, but they had stone for hearts and their eyes looked right through you or darted away. An image of the beasts being driven aboard the cattle boat on the Tonlé

Sap flashed into her mind and she feared that they too were being taken to be slaughtered. Why else would they kidnap them from their homes and take them over the border?

And now here she was in this strange city. Light was shining through the gap between the edge of the bin and the lid, so she stood up warily and pushed it open. Her breath was smoking on the air that was colder than anything she had ever known. The rain had stopped, and the sun had risen with a golden light and it was shining on the hard stuff on the pools. She'd never seen ice before. The shops were closed, but she could hear traffic somewhere behind her and in front there was a big, round-topped mountain covered in what she knew was snow from her lessons at school. Nobody was about, so she pushed the lid fully open and climbed out of the bin. She wondered if there were a wat somewhere where she could beg the monks for help. She was hungry again, so she walked over to the shops and took some more bread from a crate. It was still warm. She ate some and prayed that the shopkeepers would forgive her for stealing. She had no idea where she was going, except that she wanted to get away from the bad men, so she walked along past the shops, heading towards the mountain.

The houses here were nothing like they were at home and all the streets were covered with asphalt like she'd seen in Battambang. She relieved herself in a clump of trees and kept walking. An old man came out of a house and said something. He sounded friendly, but she couldn't understand what he said so she just smiled and kept going. When she came to a bigger road, she felt uneasy, so she stopped and climbed a fence and peered out. It was just as well, because a car drove slowly past, and she saw that the man she had hit on the head with the spanner was driving. He wasn't dead, but even though it was a sin she wished he was. She was wearing only thin shorts and a jumper with Mickey Mouse on it, with a short jacket she'd found in the bin. She was shivering and her teeth were chattering, so she climbed back over the fence and started to run, her plastic sandals slapping on the hard road that was glittering in the sunlight. A flock of black birds fluttered up in a cloud from some trees, making a strange noise like nothing she had heard before. Then a loud voice was speaking—like her father had told her about when the Khmers Rouges used loudspeakers to urge them to work harder in the fields. She slowed down because she had a stitch in her side. She walked slowly around a corner and saw the man's car. It was parked outside a shop and the man was inside buying things. There was some grassy land ahead, dotted with trees so she ran even though it hurt and got there while the man was still inside. She was in a big park, she realised, with a stream running through it, brown and angry in flood. The loud voice was coming from what looked like a school and she could see children in uniforms standing in lines and being yelled at by the loudspeaker. She followed the creek upstream and crossed over a metal footbridge into another street. There were more shops ahead, one with boxes of fruit and vegetables out the front. Maybe she could steal some fruit or maybe the shopkeeper would give her some. She was getting desperate, but anything was better than being back with those horrible men.

White people were walking briskly along the footpaths and some of them smiled at her. A tall thin man came out of the shop and started putting out more fruit for sale. He was the same colour as her, so she walked up and greeted him politely, making a temple with her hands up next to her face to show the utmost respect. He looked baffled, but he had kind eyes—big brown eyes like hers—and he said something to her in what she knew was English. He gave her a banana and she brought her hands together again and took it gratefully, thanking him profusely in her language. A woman she took to be his wife came out of the shop with a concerned look on her face. She was wearing a sari and she had a beauty spot on her face. She knelt to Nornry's level and spoke to her. Nornry didn't understand the words but her voice was kind. She would have to trust these people, so she held out her arms and the woman enfolded her on her bosom. Nornry wept and the woman made soothing noises while her husband fussed over them.

CHAPTER 28

JACK STOOD WITH LES JETSON'S PARENTS outside the mortuary chapel. The old couple had behaved with dignity while they identified their son, but Jack knew they were just holding it together. Now Les's body had been wheeled back to a mortuary cooler and they stood talking for a moment. 'I dunno what happened,' Charlie Jetson told him, rotating his best trilby in his hands. 'We remember when he was just a baby, and we were so proud. We would've done anything for him, Mr Martin, if he'd have let us.' His wife Edna silently pulled a tissue through her hands, knowing her voice would break if she spoke. Jack offered them a cup of tea or coffee, but they declined, so he shook their hands and escorted them to the exit. He watched sadly as they walked slowly up the street, supporting one another.

Simon Calvert's preliminary examination established that Jetson had been shot in the back of the head at very close range—there were powder burns round the bullet's entry point. From the trajectory, he had been kneeling, so all the signs were that it was an execution. The damage to the brain was enormous, testifying to a powerful handgun.

'I can't help you with the make, Jack,' Simon advised, 'but I'd guess it was a powerful military job. The bullet did a lot of damage while passing through.'

Duncan Snodgers, who had prised out the spent 18-millimetre bullet from the floorboards of the Glenorchy house, believed the weapon was a Makarov, the service pistol favoured by the Russian military, especially the Spetsnaz special forces soldiers. It had also been a favourite of Stalin's GPU for 'wet work'. The little Scot never ceased to amaze Jack.

After walking up Argyle Street from the mortuary, Jack stopped off at the Carlton Café for a quick coffee and a glass of water to take the taste of death from his mouth. Maxine Fowler had been found sleeping rough up on the north-east coast at St Helens and was due to arrive for an interview anytime soon. In fact, she was there already when Jack got back to the station. A uniformed officer poked his head into Jack's office and told him that she was waiting in an interview room, so he interrupted Bluey Bishop, who was filling in some forms, and they entered the room together. Maxine had lost the baby fat she had been carrying when Jack saw her last and she'd cut her curly red hair short. She stood up when they entered but Jack waved her back to her seat. He pulled his chair back a bit because she was a bit whiffy: she clearly hadn't showered for a while. Bishop fussed with the recording equipment and nodded when he got it going. His hooter wouldn't detect a sewage works during an epidemic of dysentery.

'Hello, Maxine,' Jack said kindly, with a nod of greeting. 'This is Detective Sergeant Bishop, and I am Detective Inspector

Martin. You might remember us from a few years back when we raided that Nazi place in Swan Street.'

'Yeah, I remember you, Mr Martin,' the girl replied. She was chewing on a thumbnail and her blue eyes were scatty. 'You was kind.'

She wouldn't look either of them in the face, so Jack hastened to tell her that she was not suspected of committing any offence, and that they were grateful for her tip-offs, which had enabled them to free a number of the kids from the places she'd named. However, they were anxious to find those responsible so any information she could give would help. Maxine looked like she might be about to cry, so Jack pushed a box of tissues across the table, and she took one and blew her nose. She asked if she could smoke and Jack said yeah, why not, although it was against regulations. The truth was that it was already smelly in the room and he would have an excuse to open the window for fresh air. She really needed a shower and a change of clothes.

'Now,' Jack continued, looking down at his notes, although he didn't need them. 'What can you tell us about Les Jetson, Leslie Norman Jetson.'

'Bastard!' Maxine hissed. 'Not you, Mr. Martin. 'Im! That Les. He was gunna do me in because Mr Sockinglov was angry about the Taroona place. The first one I rung you up about. That was before the others done him.'

'Let us get this straight, Maxine, you say he was going to kill you?'

'Yeah, that's right. I was hidin' an' I heard the cunt tellin' Mr Sockinglov that I was just a slag and he'd fix me good an' proper so I couldn't say nothing.'

'You must have been very scared, Maxine,' Jack observed, 'but he can't hurt you now. Now, what can you tell us about the Taroona place? We'll go back to Jetson and this Sockinglov person in a minute.' He had written 'Sockinglov???' on his notepad and underlined it several times. It was an important nugget of information.

'Well, I didn't know what was happenin' when Les first took me. He said it was a big house and he had a job there and he brung me there a few times and we … we …'

'You had sex?'

'Yeah, that's right.' She looked sheepish at this revelation, but Jack waved a hand to indicate that it was none of his business.

'How did you meet Les, Maxine?'

'It was in the pub. That place in Sandy Bay Road. The Doctor somethin' or the other.'

'The Doctor Syntax?'

'Yeah, that's the place, Mr Martin. We got talkin' in the lounge bar and I brung him back to me room in Queen Street where I was livin' then. It was a coupla months ago. I moved to Letitia Street later. I thought we was going steady, but he only wanted to f—, uh, to have sex with me when he felt like it.' She stubbed out the cigarette and looked furious at the memory. Jack wondered if anyone had ever treated this kid with respect.

'So, he would sometimes take you to the Taroona house. What did you see there, Maxine?'

'Well, at first I didn't think nothing, did I? Les told me that he was housesitting for some bloke, but I begun to wonder when I could hear kids crying underneath and he kept schtum when I asked about it. There was all this food in the freezer. Bread and stuff. Les could never have eaten it all. Cupboards was fulla stuff too. You know, baked beans an' packet soup an' stuff like that. Anyway, when he took me to the other place in Glenorchy, I knew for definite something funny was going on.'

'What sort of funny?'

'Well, there was kids there too, underneath, but Les wouldn't let me go down there. One day we was there and a car come in the driveway and Les made me hide in a cupboard. I could see out through a crack this bloke come in and said Les had to get the kids ready that night. He had a foreign accent, I dunno what sort cos I'm no good about that sorta thing. Les called him Mr. Sockinglov and was dead scared of him. I could tell. I could see why cos this Sockinglov was dead scary—I could see him now and then through a crack in the wood and I was scared I'd sneeze ...'

'Would you remember this man if you saw him, Maxine?' Jack drew a circle round the name on his pad.

'Yeah, cos he frightened me. He turned once and I could see his eyes. It was like they was dead. You know, cold, like on a fish. Anyway, how could I forget him after he shot Les?' She sniffed back tears and Jack handed her the box of tissues again.

'He shot Les?'

'Well, he made the other bloke do it, but that was later. At another place in Glenorchy, not at the Taroona place.'

'We'll come back to that, Maxine. Going back to Taroona, did you see anyone else there?'

'Well, there was this skinny bloke, a mate of Les's who come round once, mebbe twice to the Taroona place. Les called him Custard and I remember cos what kind of name is Custard? Later, Sockinglov made Custard shoot Les.'

'That's terrible, Maxine. You're sure that this one you call Sockinglov made Custard shoot Les?

'Yeah. That's right. Custard didn't want to do it, but that Sockinglov made 'im.' She shuddered and reached for the smokes. 'That was at Glenorchy, not Taroona.'

'Maxine, you're doing really well,' said Jack. 'It must be very painful for you to remember this stuff. Now, we'll come back to Custard shortly. Before you do, could you tell us if you ever *saw* the kids at all at either of the places?'

'No, I never seen them Mr Martin, because as soon as Mr Sockinglov left—I'm talking about the first time here, at Taroona, not about when Custard shot him—Les made me leave the house and walk down the hill to catch the bus back to me room. I thought about hiding to see what went on, but I didn't want that Sockinglov to see me.' She shuddered at the memory.

'Did you know why the kids were locked up there?'

'Well, I didn't at first but one day I asked Les straight out what was goin' on and he told me that they took them to a place in the city. A club. Men would pay to have sex with them. He was pissed—well, he liked his beer, Les did—and he said things he might not have done when he wasn't on the turps. That's when I decided I had to ring up about it, Mr Martin. It give me nightmares just thinking about it. I dunno where the club place was except it was in the city. Les wouldn't tell me the street or nothing, but he reckoned it was real classy.'

Here Jack made some more notes before continuing. 'Now, Maxine, you told us about the places in Taroona and Glenorchy, but do you know if there were other places where they kept kids?'

'I seen both places. Les was on the booze again one night and he reckoned there was some old factory where they brung them first and where they stored drugs. I couldn't say where it was, but I sorta got the impression it was somewhere not far from Moonah. Maybe Derwent Park? Yeah, once Les said that he had to ring Mr Sockinglov at the factory. Wait a minute … There was … Sorry, I get confused …'

'Take your time Maxine,' Jack said encouragingly as he made more notes. 'You've been doing fine.'

'Well, yeah,' she continued, lighting up another cigarette and blowing smoke up at the ceiling. 'Les reckoned there was some other place in the country. Like I say, he got drunk and was bragging like he was a bigshot instead of a dirty little bastard. That was round the time when I couldn't stand it and rung you lot. It was like a farm down there, he said. I dunno any more about it.'

'Maxine, you've been very helpful,' said Jack, writing down 'Country???' and circling it several times. 'Now, you mentioned a place they store drugs. Did you ever see it?'

'Nah, I only heard about it cos Les was boasting about it again. He said something about the Mitrepeline gang or something being finished. Mr Sockinglov had taken over. The drugs place was in the old factory I was telling you about.'

'OK.' Jack wrote down 'Mitropoulos???' on his pad. 'Now Maxine, I'd like you to do us a really big favour. I know you want to catch these people and put them away—'

'Jeez, Mr. Martin,' Maxine interrupted, 'I reckon the cunts should all be shot!'

'I can understand that Maxine, but the law doesn't allow it,' Jack explained. 'What we can do is catch them and put them away for a long time so that they can't hurt anyone else. Now, that favour I was talking about. When you've had a coffee and something to eat, we'd like you to sit down with our artist. He'll ask you a lot of questions about what Sockinglov and Custard looked like and then make drawings of them. We call it an identikit picture. We can circulate it and put it in the papers so that anyone who has seen them can help us find them.'

Maxine nodded emphatically and lit another cigarette. The air was blue with smoke.

A woman constable came to take Maxine for a meal and Jack wondered what would become of her. She was too old for fostering. Maybe, though, there was some sort of high-quality sheltered accommodation. He would have a word with one of the social workers he knew. Chances were that some other no-hoper would get his hooks into her if they didn't arrange something decent for her. Still, she had provided a great deal of information and maybe she could help them find this 'Sockinglov' character, though he doubted that was the actual name. She had also provided three other useful snippets—an old factory possibly somewhere near Moonah, maybe Derwent Park; a place in the country; and a flash club in the city. He wondered if that was the connection with the body on Shipstern Bluff. Things were starting to come together. He suddenly remembered, too, that he had the Italian lesson tonight and found himself hoping that Francesca Sorrentino would be there.

CHAPTER 29

MAD DOG BILLY BLOAT HAD BEEN OUT in the bush all night. His Drizabone coat had kept the rain and snow off but he was still freezing cold and hungry. His trousers were sopping wet, and he'd sat on some thistles and hurt his arse, so he had. He'd lost the wee sou'-wester when the wind blew it off into a ravine, so his hair was plastered to his skull. He had sheltered from the storm under an overhanging rock: not much of a shelter but better than nothing. He'd managed to sleep a bit and dream of when he'd taken Ella down to Carrickfergus in the days when they were still together. Them peelers didn't know about the pistol he'd buried, and he fingered it lovingly. It was the same model as the one he'd had back home; the one he'd killed that Croppie boy and his wee Protestant girlfriend with down at Kilkeel. It had to be done. Anyway, he'd seen coppers searching for him shortly after dawn and he'd walked a couple of miles along a creek to put the dogs off his scent. Fuck, anyone would think he was one of them outlaw rapparees—the bandits the Taigs went on about back in Ireland! A plan was congealing in his brain. When he got out of the bush, he would steal a wee car and drive down to Risdon Vale, kidnap a screw, and force them to release his cousin. Fuckin' peelers wouldn't get the better of Mad Dog! He cleared his throat and spat a gobbet of sputum into the bushes, then cocked his head. Dogs. They were tracking him with dogs, so he'd have to move fast.

The sun had come out and Billy's clothing was steaming as he made his way slowly through the dense bush. After some time, he blundered into an area of rough pastureland. Had he been less cold and tired, he might have marvelled at the extraordinary vista before him: a wide valley flanked by rearing, snow-capped mountains. He could hear the dogs barking behind him, so he forced himself onward, clambering clumsily over fences and ripping his pants on the barbed wire, his breath ragged in his throat. Cows eyed him curiously and he got a fright when a bull stood up from behind a tree and gave him a hard look. Mad Dog was an urban boy and quite out of his element here. As the land began to slope steeply downwards, a little town dotted with old sandstone buildings came into view and it gave his heart a lift. Civilisation! A wee sign at the entrance of the village told him he was entering Hamilton, established in 1835. There was no sign of human life, save for a couple of smoking chimneys, but he reckoned there would be some cars around. He had had plenty of experience hot-wiring Taig cars back home. He was bloody well starving too, so he was.

Aha! A wee ute as they called them here. Perfect. It wouldn't have none of that newfangled electronic stuff that made the new ones difficult to start. He had heard that the locals didn't lock their vehicles, but this one was locked. Still, very conveniently, someone had left some stiff wire in the gutter. After rubbing his hands together to warm them, he fashioned a loop on one end of the wire and shoved it through a wee gap at the top of the window. Patience, Billy, he muttered to himself, willing the wire to bend down towards the lock like that Geller feller did with spoons. Absorbed in the task, he didn't see the old woman come out of her house. She came up quickly behind him and demanded to know what the hell he thought he was doing. Jesus! Billy near shat himself and turned around to see her glaring at him. She had silver hair cut short and an indignant expression on her ruddy outdoors face. She was wearing blue bib and brace overalls with a flannelette shirt and had a rake in her hand. She was taller than him.

'What do you think you're doing?' she repeated in a voice that reminded him of his Ma when she was angry and about to wield the strap. Her eyes were grey and unwinking, boring straight into him.

'I err …' Billy mumbled. Then he remembered the pistol weighing down his pocket and brought it out.

The woman was outraged. 'Oh no you don't!' she snapped, raising the rake, and bringing it down smartly on Billy's hand.

Billy yelped and the pistol dropped with a clatter. He started to bend down to pick it up, but the woman was quicker, despite her years. She hooked the gun with the rake and flicked it into a nearby bush. 'Nasty man,' she admonished, 'you need to be taught a lesson!' She seized him by the front of his coat with one hand and boxed him around the ears with the other, shouting 'I'll teach you to take what isn't yours!' Billy tried in vain to ward her off, but she was relentless and stronger than him. Years of gardening and tending to her orchard and the goats had bulked out her muscles and she had always had a fiery temperament. She'd been a nursing sister before she retired and knew that men were babies. After she had given his ears a thorough battering, she grabbed him by the collar and was dragging him off down the road. 'Ye've broken me wrist, so you have,' he whimpered, wincing at the pain. Luckily for Billy, he was spared further punishment when Constable Robbie Ryan drove up in his four-wheel drive police car and jumped out grinning broadly.

'What-o, Miss Ross?' he enquired, doing his best not to guffaw. 'What scoundrel d'you have for me here?'

'This man,' she raged. 'This reprobate, I should say, was breaking into my ute. I want him charged.' She tightened her grip and cuffed Billy again. 'Keep still! He also pulled a gun on me, Constable Ryan, so you can charge him with that too.'

Ryan handcuffed Billy to an old fence but stayed close by. 'Now,' he said, pulling out pad and pencil and preparing to write. 'Let's start with your name, sunshine.'

'I'm not tullying you nothin',' Billy replied sullenly. He was embarrassed that the bloody old Amazon had bested him. 'Crazy old floozie, she's a public menace, so she is.'

Miss Ross rebuked him sharply. 'You mind your manners, sonny!' She lifted her hand and Billy hid behind the constable.

'Don't worry Mr Bloat,' Ryan laughed. 'Yes, I already know who you are.'

'Do you think you can handle him?' asked Miss Ross dubiously. 'I have to finish my weeding, and he's dangerous.' She doted on the constable and often baked him cakes and pies, worried that his mother was not there to look after him.

'Just watch him for a minute, Miss Ross,' Ryan replied. 'I'll radio through and get the Hobart people to come and get him.' Mad Dog cringed under the woman's hostile stare and hoped she wouldn't hit him again. Miss Beryl Ross, 86 years old and a confirmed spinster, didn't know it, and certainly didn't want it, but she was about to gain celebrity status not just in Tasmania but on the mainland—a place she'd visited once or twice and didn't like much.

Billy Bloat was taken to Hobart and charged. He never realised how lucky he was to be in police hands, for Sokolov was hunting him and would have put a bullet in his head as easy as eating a plate of *kasha*. The old Mitropoulos drugs firm was dead. Its dealers were either cowering in fear of further beatings or were working for the new firm. Billy's cousin had been in cahoots with the gang before he was sent down for murder and Sokolov was determined that the rival gang would stay down.

CHAPTER 30

THE BRIEFING ROOM FELL SILENT as Jack and Liz strode in. There was none of the usual shuffling and muttering. Jack went straight to the point. 'Liz will brief you on the latest developments in the "Mad Dog" saga. After that, I'll bring you up to speed on the paedophile trafficking investigation.' He took a sip of water and indicated that Liz should take over.

'As you know, a suspect was arrested yesterday at Hamilton and is "helping us with our inquiries",' she began. 'We have in custody one William Terence Bloat, aka "Mad Dog". Billy, as he likes to be known, is a 52-year-old man from Belfast in Northern Ireland.'

Here, Liz stuck Bloat's photograph up on the whiteboard. A wave of gasps and muttering broke around the room. 'Jeez,' said one, 'that's Gordon Paisley!' 'Spitting image,' opined another. 'Are we sure he hasn't escaped from prison?'

'Yes,' agreed Liz. 'He could almost pass as an identical twin, but as far as we know, they're first cousins.'

'Other side of the blanket,' joked Sergeant Fuller. 'Back it in there was hanky-panky.'

'Well, be that as it may,' said Liz, regaining the initiative. 'Mr Bloat was arrested by the local constable after a resident apprehended him trying to steal her car. Bloat pulled a gun on her, but she overpowered him and handed him over to police.

'Bloat was the subject of a police manhunt after he kidnapped a young woman and demanded a swap for Inspector Martin, here. The young woman was freed unharmed. We believe Bloat had a grudge against her for helping put his cousin away. He was also holding her and Jack hostage and demanding the release of his cousin from prison, plus a substantial amount of money, and safe passage out of the country. Clearly these demands were not acceptable, so we made the decision to free the girl and arrest Bloat if that were possible.

'As you can see, Bloat's first cousin is our former colleague, Gordon Paisley, who as you know is currently serving a life sentence in Risdon Prison for murder and other crimes. The pair of them *do* look like twins.'

Another wave of muttering and whispering spread round the room at this and Liz waited until it had subsided.

'Gordon Paisley's parents changed their name from Bloat by deed poll shortly after immigrating from Ireland. Paisley is the prisoner Bloat wanted freed.'

The room was silent, with the assembled officers drinking in the information. Most of them knew Paisley and the circumstances of his arrest some years before.

'Bloat, uh, escaped after our initial arrest'—here Liz looked more than a little uncomfortable—'and spent a miserable night in dense bush, but he is now safe behind bars. We've charged him with a number of offences, including kidnapping, and will be laying further charges shortly. These include shooting up Inspector Martin's house and bombing his car. He will appear before a magistrate tomorrow morning and we will oppose bail. She paused and scanned her notes.

'Finally, I should mention that Commander Holmes has received information about Bloat from the Royal Ulster Constabulary in Belfast. They were cagey, it seems, but they did advise that Bloat is suspected of membership of the Ulster Freedom Fighters. This group is the most extreme of the "Loyalist" paramilitary groups in Northern Ireland. He is suspected of several sectarian murders of members of the Catholic community, none of whom were mixed up in politics, or the IRA. This led to his nickname, Mad Dog.'

When Liz finished, grey-haired Senior Constable Eric Blundstone had his hand up to ask a question. She sighed quietly. The man was a dinosaur. He had been an enthusiastic 'poofter basher' in his day and was an unrepentant misogynist. He should have been pensioned off years ago but had friends at high levels.

'Is it true that the hostage is a prostitute?' Blundstone asked, causing his mates to nod approvingly. The fool was grinning as if he'd scored some kind of victory.

'Yes, she is a sex worker,' Liz replied in measured tones, staring the man down. 'However, Eric, her occupation is of no relevance whatsoever. Ms Dark is an innocent member of the public. She has suffered a frightening ordeal. She deserves protection the same as any other citizen.'

Blundstone smirked and winked to his mates. Liz ignored

him and nodded to Constable Kate Farrar whose hand was raised.

'Is it true,' Kate asked with scarcely contained glee, 'that the local resident who overpowered Mad Dog was an 86-year-old woman?'

Blundstone sneered and looked down at his feet, and Liz hoped fervently that he would have a run-in with Miss Ross. His sycophants were rolling their eyes. She recalled several of them as enthusiastic participants in the mass arrest of gay protesters some time before. The rubber glove idea might have been Blundstone's.

'Yes, that is the way it happened, Kate,' Liz agreed. 'The woman's name is Beryl Ross. She's a hero, although we should be wary of encouraging members of the public to put themselves in danger. Bloat was armed and dangerous.'

Liz sat down and Jack took over. 'OK,' he said, clearing his throat and giving Blundstone a sour look. 'As you know, we have now raided two premises and freed a number of children who were kept prisoner by an organised criminal gang. A witness has confirmed what the children themselves have told us—namely that they were hired out for sex at a club, possibly in the city. The children were kidnapped from their homes in Southeast Asia and the Balkans. It seems that we down here in Tasmania are at one end of trafficking highway controlled by an international criminal gang. We are particularly interested in interviewing a man—possibly a Russian—who seems to be called "Sockinglov", or something like that.

'As for the kids, they are currently being cared for by social services and we are liaising with police in their home countries to have them repatriated when the case is closed. Unfortunately, one of the children is seriously ill. The others have been very helpful.

'Now, the body of one of the gangsters was found out in bushland near Glenorchy. Sergeant Bishop is bringing round copies of a photograph of the dead man. His name was Les Jetson, and some of you may have come across him in your work. He was shot at close range, probably with a Russian Makarov pistol.'

Several officers raised their eyebrows and exchanged knowing glances. Jetson was most definitely 'known to the police'.

'We know from fingerprint and other evidence that Jetson was at both places where the children were kept. Now, it pains me to say this, but we have also recovered the body of a child who was buried in the garden of the Taroona property. The autopsy found that she died from a ruptured appendix and was hastily buried by her captors. She was also a few weeks into a pregnancy.' Here, a ripple of shock went round the room. Even Eric Blundstone looked appalled. Jack continued: 'We can never know the pain and terror suffered by this child. She was denied the medical care that would have saved her life. The pathologist estimates her age at no more than 13 years.

'Now, I know that you are all feeling very angry, but I can assure you that we feel confident of catching the men who have done this.'

Here Jack motioned to Bluey Bishop, who began dishing out more sheets of paper.

'We have an eyewitness who has identified two more members of the gang as being Jetson's killers. The first one, as you can see from the identikit, is a young man known by his nickname of Custard.' Eyebrows shot up around the room at this information. 'Yes, most people know him as Custard, but his real name is James, or Jamie Sproule, a North Hobart no-hoper. He seems to have graduated from illegal use of motorcars to bigger crime. Duncan and his crew have found his fingerprints in both houses. An eyewitness claims to have seen him execute Les Jetson on the orders of a man who appears to be the leader, locally at least, of the gang.

'Now, the second mug shot, which is coming round now, is of this man. Our witness knows him as Mr Sockinglov. Evidently, he's a Russian and my suspicion is that he was sent down here by his superiors to run this end of the gang's operations. From the witness's account, he is a very dangerous and frightening individual.

'We are circulating these identikit drawings and they should be appearing on television tonight and in the papers tomorrow morning. We believe that other fingerprints found at both crime scenes are his. Most likely, he ordered Custard Sproule to kill Les Jetson.'

Jack drank some water before continuing.

'Now, before we wind up and go out and catch these characters, a couple more things. I won't say any more just now, but it seems very likely that the youngster whose body we found down on Shipstern back during the summer was also a victim of this gang. We also believe that the gang might use an old factory, somewhere near Moonah. Derwent Park, maybe. So, keep your eyes peeled on that one, please.'

After the briefing, Jack met with Liz and Bluey in his office. They went over what they knew and felt confident that they were closing in on the gang.

Liz was looking thoughtful as she sipped her camomile tea. 'Look,' she said. 'I've been wondering about the real estate lot over in Melbourne who were renting out the Taroona place. I smell a rat. Let's check if they're involved with the Glenorchy place.'

Jack agreed. He'd been wondering about Taurus Holdings too. Bluey offered to do some digging to see what he could find. Further discussion was interrupted when Jack got a telephone call. 'Yes,' he said. 'Yes!' He listened and after thanking the caller he turned to his colleagues with a big smile. 'It looks like one of the kids escaped and some people rescued her.' They gulped the rest of their tea and headed for the door.

CHAPTER 31

MUNAZZA KHAN WAS A LARGE, MOTHERLY WOMAN who eschewed Western dress for the saris of her homeland. Together with her husband Sayed, she ran a mixed business in New Town, a suburb a few kilometres north of the Hobart CBD. They worked painfully long hours to ensure their children would get the best possible education and make their way in the new country. They also sent money back to impoverished relatives in Bangladesh. Mrs Khan quite lost her heart to the slight young girl who had appeared from nowhere and sought her protection. She couldn't understand a word the girl said but she gathered that she was very afraid. She took her into their parlour behind the shop while Sayed rang the police, and fed her on chicken and rice, chapatis and chutney, followed by a big bowl of fruit. 'My, you can eat,' said Munazza with a big smile, wondering where on earth the girl had come from. She'd also found the girl a jumper, jeans and woolly socks that her own kids had grown out of, so she was looking much warmer.

'Police are coming,' said Sayed, entering the room and keeping half an eye on the shop. 'They said maybe fifteen minutes. In meantime, I have our children's atlas. We will ask this girl where she is coming from.'

Munazza looked up. 'I'm hoping you told them it should be a woman officer,' she said sharply. 'I think men have been hurting this one.' She coaxed the girl into eating another banana, pushed more fizzy water over the table and glared at Sayed.

'O woman,' sighed Sayed. 'Police will send whom they please, isn't it?' He opened the atlas at the page depicting Southeast Asia and showed it to the girl. She studied it for a while, puzzling at the strange script, trying to remember what she'd learned in school. Sayed had just given up and was about to turn to a new page when the girl smiled and pointed at a little country sandwiched between Vietnam and Thailand.

'Cambodia,' he said, beaming at her. She nodded, and repeated what he said, although from her mouth it sounded a little bit different. 'There, woman,' Sayed told his wife. 'Sometimes your husband can teach you a thing or two. Now, I will inform police and they can find an interpreter for this child.'

Nornry wondered at her good fortune. She had just been about to think that she could never trust anyone again, but she just wanted to get back to her family in the kompong. She sat there contentedly though, leafing through the pages of the atlas, and in sign language asked the man called Sayed to show her where they were. Her eyes grew wide when he pointed to Tasmania and traced his finger up the page to Cambodia. When Liz Flakemore arrived with a young female social worker, Nornry backed away and clung to Munazza. She began to cry. Nothing that had happened had led her to trust white people. How was she to know that they were not friends of the bad men? She clung to Munazza and refused to leave. They were patient, however, and did not want to frighten her, so they asked Munazza if she would accompany them, and the woman readily agreed. Nornry, calmer now, held peaked hands solemnly to her face in thanks to Sayed and then followed the women out to the car.

All along the road to the city, Nornry sat cuddled up to Munazza and marvelled at what she was seeing. The women were kind to her and offered her more food when they arrived at the police station. A man came to see her too and she guessed he was a policeman even though he didn't wear a uniform. She was intrigued by his sky-blue eyes, but he seemed kind. They had been unable to locate a native Khmer speaker, and in the end, Jack rang Danny Cunningham at the university. Danny thought for a while and suggested Pierre Schumacher, a retired professor of history.

The professor was an elderly fellow who walked with a stick and had a thatch of white hair and a white spade beard. He looked doddery, but they soon found that his mind was sharp. He was a Frenchman, or more accurately an Alsatian who spoke English with a slight German accent laced with French sounds. In his youth, he had spent some years as a teacher in Cambodia, which was then a French 'protectorate'. His Khmer was rusty. 'I haven't spoken it for years and was never very good at it,' he said, but he promised to do his best.

Nornry was intrigued by the old white gentleman when he entered the room, and she stood and peaked her hands high on her face as a mark of respect to him as an old person. Schumacher returned the gesture and Nornry was delighted to hear him speaking her language, albeit with a thick accent. He accepted a cup of coffee and sat down with pad and pen to find out who she was and what had happened to her. His Khmer was indeed rusty, but it slowly came back, and she told him about the bad men who had killed the village headman and taken her and her friends. She felt that she could trust these people, but she only reluctantly agreed to allow Munazza to leave when Schumacher told her that the kind lady had to prepare dinner for her children.

CHAPTER 32

SOKOLOV DID A DOUBLE TAKE when he saw his face staring back at him from a poster outside a newsagent's shop in Moonah. It was, he had to admit, a good likeness. The nose was a trifle too long, but it was an accurate enough reproduction, even down to the livid scar on his left cheek. He was furious. It couldn't have been Jetson who had squealed. Old Trixie was too wedded to the business, so that left Jetson's tart, or Custard and his thick cousin. He'd forgotten the young man's name. He pulled up his collar and tugged his hat down further over his ears, looked round to make sure nobody had clocked him, and jumped into his car. Trixie was in the brothel's office doing the accounts when he walked in without knocking and plonked himself on the spare chair.

'We must have the words,' he said.

Trixie's little eyes narrowed when he showed her the poster he'd taken from outside the newsagent's shop. She never joked, so he was spared any stupid remarks. 'Things are really going pear-shaped,' she snapped, her Kiwi vowels strong. 'I thought you'd taken care of things but clearly we have a big problem. I'll get Alan Bull on the phone and put him in the picture.'

Sokolov got her drift and waited impatiently while she dialled Alan's number. While she was waiting for him to pick up the phone she asked what had happened to the last consignment. They were still in the factory, he said. They would be transferred to the new house Stephen had made available. But there was another big problem. Trixie put the phone down and waited for him to explain, tapping her beringed fingers on the desktop.

'One of them is escaped,' said Sokolov, shrugging his shoulders. 'A little one. Like a tiger. Clawed Sergey's face, screaming and spitting. Others are in factory still.'

Trixie screwed up her little eyes in disgust. 'How did it happen, Ivan?' she demanded.

Sokolov shrugged again. 'That one Custard and stupid cousin. They try to have fun with girls and tiger one hit Custard on head with spanner.'

'We must get Sergey the driver back and another one of the Russians from Melbourne,' said Trixie. 'These locals are useless. Chances are Custard tupped off the police to save his own skun.'

Sokolov was puzzled by the woman's Kiwi vowels and annoyed that she seemed to think she was boss. He was beginning to wonder if this *zhenshchina* wasn't getting too big for her boots. He reported to the syndicate, not this common *bordel* madam. Then again, she had a significant investment in the firm, and he could understand her concern. She was right, too. Custard and his cousin were liabilities. He patted the Makarov lovingly. It had served him well for many years and he intended it would continue to do so. He fingered his scar. A tribesman had cut him before Sokolov killed him with the Makarov.

'OK, Trixie,' he said. 'You right. We get reliabilities from Melbourne. I try to get good men, but they say to economicalise.'

'Penny wise and pound foolish. Bad policy,' Trixie noted. 'Well, we live and learn.'

Sokolov left Trixie's office and walked through the brothel, ignoring the scantily clad women lounging around waiting for custom. He'd had a few of them but had too much on his mind to be distracted. He unlocked the back door and went through into the factory, careful to secure it behind him. Custard and Sean were sitting in the old workers' lunchroom not doing anything, with their mouths open. They were idiots, thought Sokolov. Good for running errands and not much else. Well, they had used the string and were about to execute themselves. He snorted inwardly. The merchandise (save for the wildcat) was still there, lying down feeling sorry for itself on the mattresses by the back wall. Sokolov knew exactly how he was going to handle this. He would make Custard dig a grave, get him to shoot the other idiot and then execute him and roll him into the hole too. It was a good plan, and he relished the thought of finishing them off. He poked his head into the lunchroom and ordered Custard to follow him outside into the old steelyard. When he was sure they could not be overheard, he offered Custard a cigarette. They lit up and he swivelled his colourless eyes onto Custard's face.

Custard shuddered. Les had been right, Sokolov really was a Blade Runner replicant.

'We have big problem, Custard,' Sokolov said, as if taking the young man into his confidence. 'Police make drawings of you face and me faces. They now all over shops and in newspaper. It was not Les who tell police because you kill him. So, who squeal?'

The colour drained from Custard's face. 'I ain't done nothing, Mr Sokolov,' he whined. 'If you ask me, it was Les's tart Maxine who dobbed us in.'

'I think Maxine do nothing, Custard. We up how you say, poo river without a motor. What we do? You one of us. Who you think tell police?'

Custard swallowed. He didn't like the way this was going. He made another feeble attempt to blame Maxine, but Sokolov was relentless.

'No, Custard. I think you know who tell cops, but you no want to say.'

Custard felt as if a black cloud had descended over him and images of his life spooled past as if on a reel of film. He'd been to school with Sean. Played with him when they were little. Stole their first car together and pranged it at high speed on the Tasman Bridge. Done time together over in the Pink Palace. More like brothers than cousins, they always said. There'd been three of them until Mick Gorringe had run out of road one night being chased by the coppers out on South Arm. The Three Musketeers, they called themselves, like in the comic. All for one and one for all. Jesus, he cursed the day he had ever got talking with Sokolov in the bar of the Sir William Don, his North Hobart local. He'd been boozed and big-noting himself and Sokolov had offered him a job. Shouted him a feed in the Chinese next door, chow mein and all that with them roll things. Good money and nothing too hard. Easy money. Funny accent. Hadn't seen him around before but it seemed like a sure thing and Custard could handle himself.

'You know Sean squealer,' said Sokolov and Custard gave in. This man was too powerful. What could he do? Sokolov was speaking again, his voice low but full of threat. 'You go inside Custard, tell Sean come outside and we deal with problem. OK?'

CHAPTER 33

NORNRY CORROBORATED much of what the team had learned from Maxine. She reacted strongly when showed the identikit pictures of Sokolov and Custard. 'She says these are some of the men,' said Professor Schumacher. 'This one'—he pointed at Custard's mug—'made advances so she hit him on the head with a steel thing. I think she means a spanner or another tool like that.' From what she said, it seemed like the men had taken the girls to a disused steel fabrication plant. She didn't know the names of the things, but it seemed like there were steel girders on the floor and there were piles of them stacked up in the yard outside.

Maxine had mentioned an old factory, possibly in the Derwent Park area, so Jack summoned two young constables, Kate Farrar and Barney Hurst, and directed them to dress in plain clothes and take a police car and look at all the disused steel fabrication plants.

'Now, there's a couple of places on Lampton Avenue that could fit the bill,' Jack told them. 'I remember one from a few years ago, Jones something or the other. If it looks likely, do not under any circumstances attempt to enter the place. Just report straight back. These characters are murderers, and they'll react like cornered tiger snakes.'

Bluey Bishop was dogged and diligent and late that afternoon he reported what he had found about Taurus Holdings. 'Finger in a lot of pies, sir. Lots of real estate in Victoria and over here too. Incidentally, the Glenorchy place is one of theirs, or at least they manage it for an old lady who lives in New Norfolk. They are the agents for the Taroona place as we know.' He checked his notes. 'They own a winery near Geelong and another down on the Mornington Peninsula. They're into privatised utilities too. Then there are quite a few pubs and clubs and even a small engineering plant in Richmond. That's the Melbourne Richmond, sir.' Jack nodded and he continued. 'Now, where it gets interesting is that Taurus moved into the Victorian brothel industry when it was legalised a couple of years ago. They even set up a knocking shop in the old State Electricity Commission offices in the Latrobe Valley after Kennett privatised the power industry. The Victorian officer I spoke with said that he knew for a fact that they were heavily involved in illegal brothels and massage parlours before legalisation and that he suspected they still were. He was working on reports of women being trafficked into the country from Thailand. They take their passports then make them pay off the cost of their airfares and other expenses. All padded out, of course, so that the women can't escape. Sometimes they know what they're getting into, other times the poor cows think they'll be working in regular jobs. The two partners are Stephen Abercrombie and Alan Bull.' Here, Bluey pulled two glossy photographs from a folder and passed them to Jack.

'Anything you can tell me about them?' Jack asked, viewing the men's mugshots with distaste. They stank of money, arrogance, entitlement, grinning confidently and displaying perfect teeth. They spent a fortune on expensive haircuts and had never lowered themselves to wear off-the-peg clothing. The world belonged to them and they had no scruples about how they kept it that way. Women were playthings if they were young and pretty; of no account when they got older. Jack's lip curled: 'Nasty pair of private school miscreants by the look of 'em.'

'They've been operating under the radar until recently, sir,' Bluey continued. 'Yes, they have the kind of background you mention: Scotch College and Geelong Grammar, respectively. Major donors to the Liberal Party. Abercrombie's in his forties, inherited money and married into another wealthy Toorak family. Wife's name is Melissa. She's a socialite and not involved in the business as far as is known. She may even think it's all legit. Abercrombie's a show pony, though. The real boss of the show is Alan Bull. He inherited a pile and has made an enormous amount of money from shares in the mining industry as well as what we've been talking about. He's single. Forties. Never married. Keeps a low profile unlike Abercrombie and his missus who are well-known on the social scene in Melbourne. My contact thinks they are mixed up with an international trafficking gang. That's about it, sir.'

'Good work, Bluey,' said Jack. 'One thing, I wonder if either of the pair own property on the Tasman Peninsula?'

'Sorry sir, but I dunno,' Bluey replied. 'I'll do some more digging and get back to you.'

There was a stench coming off Taurus Holdings fouler than a Footscray abattoir during pig-killing season but Jack was grateful that they were on the scent, or rather the stink. He considered asking the Victoria Police to bring Abercrombie and Bull in for questioning, or flying over to do it himself, but realised that if he went at them too early, they would lawyer up and plausibly deny everything. Better to keep teasing out the loose ends first. He had also done some digging to see if he could find out anything about the so-called Mr Sockinglov, but the man was invisible. Still, the identikit might turn up something. An alert had been put out for Custard Sproule too and even if he went to ground, he would have to show himself sooner or later. Hobart wasn't that big a city that someone could vanish completely. If they were alive, that was. He was wondering, too, about the city club Maxine had mentioned. There were a few posh establishments around and the workers' club, although he doubted it would be the latter. He doubted, too, that the silvertail places would go in for it. Most likely it was a secret place set up purely for degenerates to indulge their tastes. Rock spiders, they were called. There were networks of them, he knew, telling each other that their behaviour was normal, if misunderstood.

As if on cue, Liz Flakemore knocked and entered Jack's office. She was a bit breathless from running upstairs. When she had caught her breath, the words poured out of her. 'I've just got back from driving round the city with Jana and Katarina, two of the girls from Taurus's Taroona house,' she said. 'Stefan Jovanović the interpreter was with us.

'I hoped the girls might be able to identify the building the gang took them to. Anyway, we drove around Battery Point, but the girls just shook their heads. Same with North Hobart, and New Town yielded nothing, so we drove back into the city and went up Davey Street.'

Jack thought of Davey Street, the major thoroughfare running one way up to South Hobart and beyond from the city towards the mountain. It boasted many old sandstone houses, most of which had been converted into offices, doctors' surgeries and whatnot, a couple of pubs, and the Anglesea Barracks.

'Up there with the movers and shakers eh?' he commented.

'We got lucky, Jack,' Liz continued. 'Katarina sort of quivered like a pointer and put her hand to her mouth. The two girls whispered together, and Stefan translated. "It's there!" he said. "The big stone and brick place on the right." I pulled in a bit suddenly, er, might have upset one or two of the motoring public. I think I did hear a horn or two.

'I jumped out and took a look at the place. It was big alright. A laneway went round by the side to what appeared to be a carpark out the back. Front door was up some sandstone steps, with this polished brass plate on the door, saying it's the Van Diemen Club.'

'Well might you say Figjam, Liz,' said Jack, passing her a

mug of tea and a biscuit from his private stash. He'd vaguely heard of it; a posh establishment that kept a low profile, did not admit women and was secretive about its membership. 'Bloody marvellous work! Let's say we pay this Van Diemen mob a visit tomorrow morning and see what we can find.'

Liz went quiet. 'They're such nice kids, Jack. I bought them an ice cream before dropping them back at the shelter, but it just seemed so bloody inadequate after what they've been through. You'd think I'd given them the moon, though.'

Jack passed her his clean handkerchief.

CHAPTER 34

CUSTARD WAS CRYING. He was standing in the factory yard in the dwindling winter light sobbing his heart out. 'I can't do it, Mr Sokolov,' he snivelled. 'Sean's me best mate.'

Sokolov's usually immobile face screwed up in a scornful rictus. '*Pizda!*' he sneered. 'What you, man or fuckin' pussy?'

He forced Sean to kneel beside the open grave he had ordered Custard to dig in a far corner of the yard. The long-handled shovel was flung to one side. They had struck rock and the grave was shallow. Custard was holding the Makarov with its long silencer in a trembling hand blistered from the digging.

'Please, mister,' Sean whimpered. 'I never done nothing.' He had wet himself. Sokolov's saurian eyes showed no emotion. Sean began to mutter a prayer, trying to remember the words that the Religious Instruction teacher had tried to instil into his skull back at New Town High.

Custard's gun hand was shaking violently, and he wiped away his tears with the other one.

'I tell you, pull trigger!' shouted Sokolov. 'Crying like girl!'

Custard obeyed, but the shot went wide and ricocheted off one of the girders lying in the yard. The racket of the nearby concrete plant muffled any noise from the silenced pistol.

'Last time,' warned Sokolov. 'Shoot him or I kill *you!*'

Something snapped inside Custard's brain. It suddenly dawned on him that he was armed and Sokolov wasn't. He wheeled round and shot his tormentor in the leg. Sokolov howled with pain but started to hobble towards Custard, swearing in Russian. Sean, meanwhile, had stood up quickly. He grabbed the pistol from Custard, aimed two-handed as he had seen on TV thrillers, and shot Sokolov smack in the middle of his forehead. They stood transfixed for several minutes, their eyes staring and huge in the gathering dusk. It was like they had got rid of a demon, like in *The Exorcist*, Sean thought. Snapping out of their trance, they moved together and rolled Sokolov's lifeless body into the grave he had meant them to share. He was surprisingly heavy, his body oddly floppy. He lay there, four feet down on his back, open-eyed with a look of surprise still on his face.

'Quick, let's bury the cunt,' said Custard, so Sean fetched another long-handled shovel from the sand-blasting shop. 'Wait,' Custard ordered, bending down to pick up the Makarov. Showing surprising presence of mind, he used his T-shirt to thoroughly wipe it clean of fingerprints. Then he jumped down into the grave and pushed the weapon into Sokolov's lifeless hand. 'Right, Sean,' he said, climbing out. 'Let's cover the arsehole up.'

The two young men worked frantically to fill in the shallow grave, sweating despite the chill. When they had finished, they tamped down the earth with the backs of their shovels and carried some of the lighter girders over to cover up the grave. They should prevent animals from digging Sokolov up, Custard reckoned. 'Let's hope he don't come back like in *Night of the Living Dead*,' said horror film buff Sean. When they were finished, they threw the shovels back into the sand-blasting shop and wondered how to get out of the place. They didn't dare go through the brothel for fear of running into Mrs Ashford, who had a Smith and Wesson pistol in her desk, so they climbed over the side fence regardless of the barbed wire. Free, they jumped into Custard's old EH Holden and fishtailed along Lampton Avenue in their haste to escape. Old Ma Ashford peered out through her office window. The smoke from burning rubber hung in the air.

'Bloody hoons,' she tutted. 'Bad for business. Must get on to the council to put in judder bars.'

She went back to counting her money. Money. What was it in that song, 'money makes the world go round'? Yeah, that was it. Trixie was worried about the way things were going but was determined to hang on to what she had. Claw her way back to where she was with the flash Davey Street brothel. Never had nothing for free. Grown up on that hopeless farm near Ranfurly in central Otago where it was either hot as buggery or it'd freeze your arse off in winter. They never had nothing, and the smell of the fried mutton chops they'd lived on still turned her guts. Them and pullets' eggs, half rotten half the time. Black pudding and lumpy old porridge. Still couldn't come at it. There was some brothers and sisters, but she'd almost forgotten their names. Dad was gaunt and silent; come back from the war not quite all there in the head. Spent their money on Mr Speight's ales in the bar of the Lion Hotel and would come back mean as catshit and reach for the strap or use his fists on them. Her mother done nothing to stop him; she was worn down like an old shoe. When Trixie turned 12, she was crutching sheep and hardly went to school. For some reason she always remembered her mother hanging out sheets she'd washed by hand, gazing at the Hawkdun Mountains, sniffing at the smell of snow in the air. Fuck knows what she thought was over them mountains! When Trixie turned 16, they had started making noises about her marrying old Murray Worsop who lived over at St Bathans, so she'd run away and had never gone back. Never heard from them again. She'd made it to Auckland, where she'd hung round the Great Northern Hotel and turned her first tricks for an Australian pimp they called Wombat Spencer. She'd got sick of the bastard taking all her money, so she'd persuaded a sailor on one of the Union Steamship boats to stow her away. From Sydney she'd made her way to Melbourne, still turning tricks, but as her own boss. She was on top now. She wasn't pretty anymore but she didn't need to be. She'd take her money and piss off, maybe back to New Zealand.

CHAPTER 35

CONSTABLES KATE FARRAR AND BARNEY HURST drove slowly down Lampton Avenue, peering left and right at the facades of the warehouses and factories, proud to be in plain clothes, up there with their heroes in the CIB. Many of the buildings they passed were derelict, victims of the Paul Keating globalisation mania that had swept the country and stopped it making things. They passed a concrete plant that was in full swing, with lines of agitator trucks queueing to receive a batch of the liquid rock.

'Hey,' said Barney, indicating that Kate should stop. 'Look at that place on the right there. You can still make out the sign: "Jones Firebird Steel Fabrication & General Engineering".'

Kate stopped and they peered out the driver's side window. The front of the premises was a yellow brick office block, but behind it was a tall industrial building clad in corrugated iron. The double side gates were secured with a strong padlock. It was shiny and must have been in frequent use. Stacks of steel girders were dotted around the outside yard, above which was a rusting overhead crane.

'Yeah, this is it,' said Barney. 'Let's ring the bell out the front and see if anyone's home.'

Kate demurred. She was less impulsive than Barney. 'Nah,

better not,' she replied. 'Remember what the Inspector said. We're to radio it in and await instructions.'

Jack nodded approvingly when word came about the place, and it didn't take long before he knew its history. The factory had once been a thriving steel fabrication shop, manufacturing heavy steel girders and other parts for bridgework, high-rise buildings, and industrial installations. It was very much like the place where Gordon Paisley's father had worked as a welder. Most likely it was the same place that a gang had demanded ransom money be dropped off at a few years back. It had been completely deserted back then. The Jones Firebird Pty Ltd plant had closed during a recession and never reopened. The company still owned it, but an agent had let it out to a Mrs Mavis Witherspoon. The agent could not say what Mrs Witherspoon with her blue-rinse hair used it for but was just happy that it was rented out. Plenty of other old factories were just rotting these days, waiting to be knocked down and replaced with shopping malls and the like selling stuff made overseas that used to be made right here. Farrar and Hurst had not found any other likely premises, so Jack made the decision to raid the place.

It was dark when they drove into Lampton Avenue. Jack noticed a couple of BMWs and Mercedes parked by the kerb. They were as out of place in this neighbourhood as Gina Rinehart or John Howard at the Trades Hall. Bluey hammered on the front door of the offices and Jack rang the doorbell repeatedly. Nobody answered, but there were subdued lights on inside, visible through the frosted glass door. Jack nodded and a uniformed constable swung the enforcer at the lock. It shattered at the first blow and Jack ran inside, holding his service pistol. It was a knocking shop. Young women were scampering about in various stages of undress and there were some red faces when officers burst into the cubicles lining the corridor. In one cubicle, a well-known businessman was dancing about on one leg trying to climb into his trousers. In another an old Labor Party heavy was sitting on the bed with a resigned look on his face. Next door, Bluey Bishop saw a bare foot sticking out from under the bed, on which a naked young woman was sitting giggling nervously. 'OK,' ordered Bluey. 'Out!' He kicked the foot, eliciting a groan. 'Well blow me down,' laughed Bluey as the smooth features of a Liberal Party mover and shaker emerged. The man stood, rummaged through his trouser pockets, and produced a sheaf of notes, which he held out to Bluey.

Jack entered at that moment and shook his head in mock sadness. 'Attempting to bribe an officer of the law is a serious offence,' he said. 'Sit there, sir, until we tell you otherwise.'

Trixie Ashford, the madam, was sitting at her desk eyeing the police. She'd been arrested more times than an octogenarian had had breakfasts, so there was no particular expression on her heavily made-up face. Indeed, she had slathered the make-up on so thickly that it might have cracked if she smiled, not that this was a frequent occurrence.

'Hello, hello, hello, Trixie!' teased Jack, sniffing the air and wagging a finger at the woman. 'We meet again, but you know, I could swear you've been burning things.'

'Just smoking a cigarette,' Trixie replied, making to push a ceramic bowl under the desk with her foot.

'You've been burning evidence,' Jack retorted, pushing her to one side and pulling out the bowl. The madam had been burning paper. 'We'll see if Mr Snodgers can make anything of this. Now, if you're agreeable, Trixie, you can give me a tour of the premises.'

Trixie fixed him with her mean little eyes and told him to look for himself, but Jack insisted. 'I want you out of this office, now, and you are not to try to come back in.' The woman looked as if she were about to arch her back and hiss, but she complied and stood in the corridor with a defiant look on her face, contumacious as ever.

'Now, Trixie,' Jack said, looking at a door at the end of the corridor. 'What's down there?'

'Dunno,' she replied. 'Never been there.'

'Liar,' said Jack. 'Where's the key?'

'Never been there, I'm telling you. I don't have no key neither.'

'Tsk, tsk, Trixie, double negatives again,' Jack chided. He turned to a uniform. 'Watch her,' he ordered, before signalling to another officer to bring the enforcer. 'Now Trixie, this will be a real Pandora's box, old girl.'

The door was much more solid than the glass thing out the front, which was as flimsy as the negligees on Trixie's employees, so it took several blows with the enforcer before it opened with a blast of ice-cold air. Jack stalked through and found himself in the cavernous interior of the fabrication shop. He located a light switch and a line of industrial lights snapped into life. Two or three overhead cranes were stationary along a runway some thirty feet above the concrete floor, and steel girders were still lying where they had been left when the premises closed. Down the far end of the building, they found five skinny children huddled together on some thin mattresses. It was freezing and Jack wondered why they hadn't succumbed to exposure. They were around the same age as Nornry. None of them spoke English, but Jack assumed that they too were Cambodian. They were terrified, but Jack spoke softly, and they seemed reassured although they could not understand the words. Two female officers took over. 'Get Professor Schumacher out here, pronto,' said Jack, dusting the knees of his trousers and walking over towards a set of stairs leading up to some offices set above the shop.

The offices were deserted, although there was an overflowing ashtray on the desk and other signs of recent occupation. A Gore-Tex rain jacket hung on a peg, and there were unwashed mugs sitting on the draining board of a sink. The room next door was padlocked shut, so an officer came up with bolt-cutters and snipped off the lock. The electricity was still on so Jack pulled on a pair of latex gloves and flipped the switch. 'Christ,' he muttered, surveying the boxes full of bags of heroin, and the blocks of hashish neatly stacked on the shelving that ran round the walls. It was full as a Jardine Matheson storehouse during the Opium Wars, but whoever was behind it did not trade By Appointment to Queen Victoria's descendant.

There was no sign of Sockinglov, nor of Custard, and Mrs Ashford professed never to have heard of them. She appeared indifferent. Arrests, fines, and periods of imprisonment were overheads in her line of business. She hardly took any notice when Jack told her she was a perennial disappointment. She'd do her time and take her money and set up in a pub in Auckland or Dunedin. Retire in comfort. She was bundled into a police car and driven down to the central police station and lodged in what the duty sergeant assured her was a nice little cell. Officers ran crime scene tape around the old factory. After speaking with Professor Schumacher, the children were taken into care.

Later that evening, Bellerive police arrested Custard Sproule and Sean Hurd. A suspicious Greek shopkeeper had seen them pocketing eggs and other items from his shelves and had come up behind them and smacked their pockets. The eggs broke and the man and his wife and adult son kept the pair at bay with pepper spray until the police arrived. Mr and Mrs Fiotakis already knew who Custard was because his face was staring out from the newspapers sitting on their front counter. The police chose not to notice the pepper spray, which was illegal.

Jack made it to the Italian class in good time. The dragon hadn't arrived, but Francesca was already there. She patted the seat next to her. 'Well, you've been a busy boy, Jack,' she said. 'I've been following your cases in *The Mercury*.' She had a very level, direct gaze, and a warm smile. They chatted easily until Ms Locatelli swept in and wrote ESSERE in big letters on the whiteboard without breaking her stride. Dragon or not, she was one of the most energetic people Jack had ever met. Francesca smiled and turned her attention to her notebook. 'Essere!' declaimed Ms Locatelli. 'The infinitive of the Italian verb to be! An essential building block of the language! Now who remembers how to conjugate the present tense?' Her severe blue eyes focussed on Jack and he was thankful that he'd managed to do his homework. After the Italian lesson, Francesca said that she had to rush to pick up her children. Jack didn't dare ask if she had a partner, but he very much hoped she hadn't. He realised that he had forgotten about work—something that was all too rare an occurrence in his life. Francesca, he thought, what a beautiful name.

CHAPTER 36

JACK AND BLUEY ENTERED THE INTERVIEW ROOM at 9:15 on a chilly winter's morning. The heating was playing up so they'd kept their jackets on. It didn't seem to faze Custard Sproule, who was slumped on a metal chair staring out vacantly through the reinforced glass window and picking his nose. His lawyer, a posh young woman who introduced herself as Fiona Browne 'with an e', was seated next to him, not looking entirely comfortable with either the ruffian's propinquity or her chair. Jack sized her up: Redchapel Avenue, Fahan School, the university law school, followed by virtually automatic employment in an old established chambers with brass plate and sandstone premises in the city. She was nervous; probably her first real case. Unlike some other coppers, Jack did not view defence lawyers *ipso facto* as the enemy, and he was gracious with her, inquiring whether she had been offered tea or coffee. People such as Custard Sproule were entitled to legal representation, whatever Fuller and Langdale thought of that. Bluey started the recording machine and they introduced themselves. Jack explained Sproule's rights and he acknowledged that he understood.

'Now Jamie,' Jack began. 'Or do you prefer Custard?' Custard shrugged, so Jack continued. 'Jamie, the charges against you are very serious, so I'd advise you to be completely honest with us.' Custard looked incapable of honesty, but Jack had to try. 'You are charged with kidnap, unlawful imprisonment, and trafficking minors for the purposes of sexual exploitation, and aiding and abetting rape.' He added, as if an afterthought, but it was calculated: 'Oh, and the murder of Les Jetson.'

Custard had appeared to be half asleep, but his eyes shot open at the mention of a murder charge and the hardboiled expression had been wiped off his face. You could see his brain whirring behind his eyes as he tried to work out how Jack knew about Les.

Jack noted his reaction and continued. 'It is also possible that you will be facing further charges relating to the deaths of several children, and to trafficking in Class A drugs. Quite a charge sheet, you'll agree. So, I repeat, while you are looking at a very long prison sentence, it is in your own interests to be completely honest with us. So, Jamie, do you understand the nature of the charges against you?'

'Yeah,' mumbled Custard, looking dazed. At this point Ms Browne requested to confer with her client in confidence. Jack agreed and he and Bluey left the room. Ten minutes later, the session resumed.

'My client wishes to state,' said Ms Browne, pushing the heavy black frames of her glasses further up her pointy nose, 'that although he admits to being involved with the unlawful detention, he had nothing whatsoever to do with children's deaths and that he was forced to kill Mr Jetson. He is not an important person in this whole unfortunate business and is more of a victim than anything else. We rather hope that because Jamie has agreed to cooperate fully this will be considered during sentencing.'

'OK,' Jack nodded. 'So may we assume that your client will cooperate fully with our investigation?'

Ms Browne nodded to Custard and he agreed to tell everything he knew. He insisted that he and his cousin Sean were minor players in the racket. The important people were 'a foreign bloke called Sokolov' and 'that old cow Mrs Ashford. Trixie. Me and Sean just done what we was told.' There was a driver, another foreigner called 'Surgee or somethin' like that', and 'sometimes they seen a bloke in a suit come into the factory'. He didn't know the Suit's name, but he had taken him to the airport once and he thought he was from Melbourne. Yeah, he would recognise him. 'He was a flash sorta bloke in a thousand-dollar suit with a red tie.' He didn't know where to find the man he called Surgee. 'He'd come and go, drivin' an' that', he explained and insisted that Sokolov told him nothing. Sokolov ordered him to shoot Les Jetson because he'd tipped off the coppers about the kids. He thought this was maybe through his girlfriend, a 'redhaired slapper called Maxine'.

'Stop here, Jamie,' Jack interrupted, restraining his indignation over the way Custard talked about Maxine. 'We have a witness who will testify that you shot Les Jetson.'

'Sokolov made me, Mr Martin,' Custard insisted. 'He was gunna do me if I didn't do Les. Honest.' The last time he had seen Sokolov was at the factory. He and Sean were getting toey about the whole business and they 'was real scared' that Sokolov would 'do them in'. As he told it, Sokolov was a homicidal maniac. He'd chewed throats out with his steel teeth over in some place Custard had never heard of before. Him and Sean had climbed over the fence and legged it to Sean's flat. Their intention was to try to get over to Melbourne, but they'd got caught shoplifting because they didn't have any money. Maybe they would have 'done some burgs to get the airfares', he admitted. Sean Hurd corroborated what Custard had said and they both agreed to help the artist produce an identikit drawing of the man in the suit. They readily identified Sokolov from the drawing prepared from Maxine's description of the man: 'Yeah, that's him.' Nevertheless, Jack had the gut feeling that they were not telling him all that they knew.

Trixie Ashford stared at Jack with her cruel little eyes and flatly denied having anything to do with the trafficking. She had never set foot in the factory, she claimed, and only knew Sokolov because she sub-let the front offices from him. Challenged about the identity of Mavis Witherspoon, she shrugged and said she'd never heard of her. She would put her hand up to running a house of ill repute, but nothing more. She did not approve of paedophilia or rape, she insisted. She ran a clean house and if she were running the same business in Melbourne, it would be perfectly legal, she said, putting on a show of indignation. Jack snorted. The woman had no conscience and no empathy. She only cared for money and there wasn't much she wouldn't do to get it. They would detain her without bail while investigations continued. Jack knew she was lying because Custard and Sean claimed to have seen her in Sokolov's office and he believed them. The woman was a serpent—unusual in someone from the land of the long white cloud, but a snake, nevertheless.

'How do the drugs and kids get here?' Jack demanded, but she stonewalled, claiming to know nothing about any trafficking racket and in the end, he had to give up. A lesser liar would have confessed when presented with evidence that she had been in the factory, but Trixie Ashford stuck to her guns.

On the other hand, Jack had no reason to disbelieve the claims of the young women who worked for her not to know anything of what went on in the factory. Indeed, they seemed genuinely shocked about the trafficking. One of them, a short blonde called Samantha Towns, who looked mid-twenties but turned out to be 18, said that Sokolov had been a client. All the girls were frightened of him, she said. There was something nasty and cruel about him. His eyes had no real colour—'it was like they was dead,' she said with a shudder. She also claimed to have seen another man they called the Suit come through the front and go out into the factory. She didn't know his name or where he came from, and though he sometimes availed himself of the girls he'd never had her. She was reluctant to say that she'd seen Trixie Ashford going through into the factory, but after Jack questioned her at length, she admitted that it was the case. She seemed like a nice kid, so Jack wondered about giving her some advice to get off the game but figured that it was none of his business.

Sokolov had disappeared, perhaps because his face was all over the papers and the TV, and there was no sign of the man Custard and Sean called Surgee—Jack figured they meant Sergey. Soon his features were widely circulated too. Duncan Snodgers had orchestrated a major search of the old factory for forensic clues and as Trixie Ashford's fingerprints were all over the office and storeroom in the factory, she was looking at serious gaol time.

One morning Bluey knocked on Jack's door grinning broadly. 'Sir,' he said excitedly. 'Interpol just came through about that Sokolov bloke. He's a real bad piece of work, alright. His real name's Ivan Smirnov.' He stopped to consult his notes. 'He's 45 years old and wanted back in Russia for a string of Mafia-related murders and other crimes. He was, let me see … born in Moscow and is an Afghanistan war veteran … Fought with the Spetsnaz special forces. Seems when he got back home, he fell in with the wrong crowd.'

'Yeah, you're right, Bluey,' Jack replied.

Jack had read widely on the fall of Communism and its aftermath and could sketch out the bones of Sokolov/Smirnov's post-war life. He would have been restless and could not settle back into the humdrum routine of civilian life. The chaos and the burgeoning of shady '*biznizmeni*' that came with the rise of Boris Yeltsin would have given him ample scope for excitement and profit. Never attached to communist ideals, or disillusioned, he would have taken to a life of crime like a Muscovy duck to the Volga.

'There's a big reward out for him in Russia,' Bluey added. 'Lots of roubles, I reckon.'

'Anything there that would give a clue about how he was able to enter Australia?'

'Nah,' replied Bluey, worrying at a fresh zit. 'Don't say nothing about it here.'

Jack's hunch was that he had used the same 'private' route used to smuggle the kids and drugs. Then again, the Russian Mafia could get their hands on false passports—or doctored ones—without difficulty.

Later that day, Bluey was back, so excited that he couldn't sit still and kept tripping over his words.

'Spit it out,' said Jack, grinning broadly.

'Well, sir,' said Bluey, passing over a sheaf of paper. 'Melbourne CIB have just sent us these: copies of photographs showing Sokolov—or Ivan Smirnov—dining with the Taurus partners, Stephen Abercrombie and Alan Bull.'

'Who's this?' Jack asked, tapping the mugshot of a fourth man; a hard-faced bruiser who was evidently proposing a toast. There was a younger man there too, keeping in the background.

'That's Nikolai Kuznetsov,' said Bluey. 'Leastways that's the name he trades under. According to Interpol, his name's, let's see, Afanasy Popov.' He leafed through some notes. 'He's another former Spetsnaz soldier, evidently was a colonel. Native of St Petersburg.'

'Excellent,' said Jack, and Bluey grinned like a puppy about to be rewarded with a biscuit. 'Now, who's the young bloke in the background?'

'Oh yairs,' replied Bluey. 'Interpol says he's Sergey Petrov.'

Jack raised his eyebrows. 'Could be the one Custard Sproule calls "Surgee"; the driver who delivered the kids and drugs to the Lampton Avenue factory, and who picked up kids at night after they'd been to the sex club in the city.'

After again thanking his sergeant, Jack got straight on the telephone to the CIB in Melbourne. It was time to strike hard. Abercrombie and Popov were arrested in dawn raids in Toorak. Sergey Petrov, however, was nowhere to be found. Later that afternoon, Jack and Bluey were sitting on a plane to Melbourne and went straight by taxi to the CIB offices to interview the suspects.

Popov glowered when they entered the interview room. He had been a handsome young man once, Jack could see; sharp Slavic features and intelligent blue eyes, and a trim physique. Jack could picture him in Red Army full dress uniform turning heads on the Nevsky Prospekt, bursting with pride in his role as a defender of the Socialist Motherland; a member of the army that had lifted the siege of Leningrad and smashed the Nazi beast in its lair. Now, many years later, the former Colonel's hair was still thick, if grey, but his face had coarsened, his mouth was a thin, cruel line, and there was no warmth in his predatory eyes. Any ideals and principles he once had had been burned out of him. The old adage, 'show me the boy and I'll give you the man', did not hold with this gangster.

They began the recording, but Popov refused to confirm his identity. '*Bez kommentariyev*'—'no comment', and '*nyet*'—'no', seemed to be the extent of his vocabulary as he sat eyeing Jack and Bluey sardonically, sucking periodically on his cigarette. He greeted questions about Sergey Petrov with a shrug. He knew better than to squeal and risk a shiv in the neck in some prison yard, and after a while Jack gave up, and Popov was led off to the cells.

Night had fallen and after a desultory meal picked at in the police canteen, Jack and Bluey interviewed Stephen Abercrombie. Abercrombie managed to look both cowed and indignant at the same time. Despite the expensive teeth and clothing, he was looking decidedly scruffy, and Jack took great delight in imagining how he would look dressed in dirty overalls and high-vis jacket. His silver-framed glasses were smeared—perhaps he had been crying—and he was badly shaven. His solicitor stood up and shook hands. A dapper little chap called Tobias Nightingale; he immediately began to sing. 'My client wishes to state that he is completely innocent', he said. 'He is a respectable businessman from an impeccable family—'

'Yes, very well, Mr Nightingale', interrupted Jack. 'All in good time, please.'

After the usual preliminaries, Jack focused on the suspect, who appeared to have perked up a bit after his lawyer's testimonial. 'They call you the Suit', he began, and Abercrombie's face wilted.

'I object to this line of questioning,' said Nightingale, wagging an accusatory finger. 'I fail to see why you are asking my client about some preposterous nickname.'

'Because,' Jack replied, 'that's what witnesses to some very serious crimes call your client.'

Eventually, despite constant interruptions by Nightingale, Abercrombie admitted that he had been to the Lampton Avenue factory in Hobart but only because he was interested in buying the place.

'My client,' piped up Nightingale, 'is already the part-owner of an engineering plant in Melbourne and wants to expand interstate.'

Abercrombie admitted that Alan Bull was his business partner but claimed to know little if anything about his personal life. 'Alan keeps pretty much to himself,' he said. 'We do meet socially from time to time, but I wouldn't call us friends.' He insisted that had never met or even heard of Afanasy Popov or Nikolai Kuznetsov, and the same went for Trixie Ashford, Ivan Sokolov/Smirnov and Petrov. He persisted even when Jack told him he had a witness who would testify to his dealings with Sokolov/Smirnov and Ashford.

At this point, Jack nodded to Bluey, who leaned forward and laid a sheaf of photographs fanwise across the desk. 'For the benefit of the tape,' said Bluey, 'I am showing Mr Abercrombie a series of photographs that show him eating dinner and drinking wine with Popov and Ivan Smirnov, alias Ivan Sokolov, along with Sergey Petrov.'

Abercrombie slumped in his chair. Jack nodded again, and Bluey read the man his rights and formally charged him with a series of crimes including trafficking children and drugs and being an accessory to rape and murder. He was remanded in custody and Jack started proceedings to have him extradited to Tasmania.

Abercrombie's Taurus Holdings partner, Alan Bull, was not at his office in the Melbourne CBD and nor was he at his Toorak mansion. The staff at both places said that he had not been seen for some weeks but that this was not unusual as he would often stay at his beachfront house near Byron Bay or at his Tasmanian property. The NSW police reported that Bull was not at Byron Bay and Jack's colleagues could not locate where he might be in Tasmania. Jack, however, had a good idea of where the property was. Although Bull had covered his tracks so well that Bluey Bishop had been unable to track down his Tasmanian address, Jack suspected it was somewhere on the Tasman Peninsula, an irregular mass of broken land poking out into the sea east of Hobart, separated from the Forestier Peninsula and the Tasmanian mainland by the impossibly narrow Eaglehawk Neck. He flew back to Hobart keen to resume the hunt.

CHAPTER 37

LIZ AND JACK STOOD SHIVERING on the front steps of the Van Diemen Club. A freezing wind was gusting down Davey Street, scattering leaves and rubbish before it. Liz pressed the entry phone, and a distorted voice asked their business, sounding like something out of Doctor Who. The door screamed 'money!'—glossy black enamel paint, a Georgian fanlight, and a discreet brass plate like the ones on the specialist doctors' surgeries nearby. There was a click and the door swung open on oiled hinges. A corpulent figure was framed in the light from the corridor behind. 'Enter, please,' the figure invited. The voice was throaty, posh Lower Sandy Bay. He cleared his throat and stood aside to let them in. 'Ahem, we're men only here but we'll make a dispensation for you, my dear,' he informed Liz. 'You may hang your coats on the pegs behind you, but first may I see some ID?'

They flashed their warrant cards and Jack gave their names. Satisfied, the man waddled slowly down the corridor and they followed. He was wearing casual clothes but hadn't bought them at Kmart: bespoke, Jack reckoned. He ushered them into his office.

'Take a seat,' he invited, gesturing towards some Chesterfield armchairs. 'I'm Morrison Hunt, the club secretary.' He steepled his chubby fingers and regarded his visitors over the top of his black-rimmed bifocals before glancing at the large wall clock meaningfully. Jack and Liz exchanged looks.

'Now, what can I do for you?' Hunt asked briskly. He had a supercilious look about him that Jack disliked. There would be a Hutchins or Grammar Old Boys tie in the corner closet, Jack knew. Hanging in pride of place on the wall was a framed testamur for a business studies degree from Bond University.

Hunt was looking at his watch again. He was ignoring Liz, so Jack lifted an eyebrow and Liz took the cue. 'Mr Hunt,' she said, 'we have had complaints that these premises have been used for immoral purposes.' She put air quotes round the allegation and waited for his response. Both officers watched him carefully, looking for clues from his body language. They let the silence hang and eventually Hunt spoke.

'My dear young lady,' he said, his porcine features giving nothing away. 'That is a preposterous allegation. We run a tight ship here, I can tell you. No riffraff; only the great and the good, as it were.' He swivelled his face from one to the other with the merest soupçon of a smile on his lips.

'Nevertheless,' Liz replied, deliberately exaggerating her Strine accent. 'You'll understand that we have to take these allegations seriously, so you won't mind if we take a quick look around.' It was a statement, not a question.

'May I ask who made these allegations?' Hunt asked.

They ignored him. 'As my colleague has said,' Jack prompted, 'we would like to look round.'

'No question of a warrant?' said Hunt with a smug look on his face.

'We were rather hoping for your cooperation, sir,' said Liz smoothly. 'If there's nothing to these allegations, I'm sure that you will be only too happy to help us.'

Hunt gave a thin smile. 'As you wish. But perhaps before I give you the grand tour you would like tea or coffee?'

'Thank you,' Jack replied. 'That is kind of you. Coffee for me. Milk and two sugars.'

Liz shook her head. 'Nothing for me, thank you.'

Hunt pressed the intercom on his desk and made the order. He sat back in his chair and opened his arms expansively. 'Now, while we're waiting, please feel free to ask anything about the club. I must say, it's jolly cold today, so I hope we're warm enough for you.'

'Fine, thanks,' Liz replied. If anything, the room was over-heated. 'We've been wondering about the Van Diemen Club. We know about the Athenaeum, the Tasmania Club and so forth, but you keep a very low profile. Any reason for that?'

Hunt steepled his fingers again and gazed at Liz, his eyes magnified like boiled eggs by his glasses. 'We are very choosy, Miss. The kind of people we value know about us and that's what matters. We're not interested in advertising ourselves to the hoi polloi.'

'Like us,' thought Liz, trying not to show her dislike of the man. He was a cocky bastard. Used to getting his way. 'OK,' she said, 'and what kind of people are we talking about here? Oh, and by the way, it's Detective Sergeant.'

'Very well, *Detective Sergeant*,' Hunt replied evenly, spreading his hands, and smiling condescendingly. 'We accept only the best men in society really. La crème de la crème, I venture to say. Many of our members are from old established families; people who can trace their ancestry right back to the Old Country. No convicts perching in family trees, I can assure you! We have quite a few Midlands landowners, families here since the Year Dot. Then there are medical specialists, topflight politicians of the right persuasion, the cream of the legal profession, old money, established businessmen. Get the picture?' They did. 'Oh,' he added with a toothy smile, 'and as you will have noticed, we do not admit women. More trouble than they're worth, really.'

Liz realised it was a lame attempt at a joke and gave an exaggerated smile.

Hunt kept smiling. 'And may I ask,' he said in a lower tone, 'which, ahem, school you attended Inspector?'

'Murray High School, Queenstown,' Jack replied roundly.

'Ah,' said Hunt with a slight smirk. 'Anyway, refreshments have arrived.' Liz's school did not rate a question.

A middle-aged butler had entered discreetly, bearing a silver tray. While Hunt waffled on about the weather and men of good breeding, the butler set out coffee jug, teapot, milk, sugar, cups and saucers, shortbread biscuits and macaroons on the corner of Hunt's large mahogany desk. The tea set looked like a Wedgwood original, thought Jack. Like the one Helen had left. Real silver spoons too, and the biscuits weren't Arnott's.

'Been here long, sir?' he asked the butler.

'Oh, the best part of thirty years, I should say, sir,' the man replied, pouring the tea and coffee. 'Now, if there's nothing else, I'll leave you gentlemen—and the lady—to your business.' With that he left, gliding across the expensive carpet on rubber-soled shoes.

'That's Evans,' said Hunt, taking a macaroon and dipping it in his Earl Grey. 'Worth his weight in gold, I must say. Quiet, efficient, and respectful. He'll have to be pensioned off someday and it will be hard to find a suitable replacement.' He took a bite of his biscuit and raised his eyebrows in appreciation. When they had finished their drinks, he stood and motioned them to the door. 'Shall we do the tour?'

Everything was understated luxury: handsome prints and a few oil paintings dating from colonial times, including an original Glover if Jack wasn't mistaken; expensive wallpaper, fine old clocks, a surprisingly modern kitchen, high double-glazed windows with views of snow-capped Mount Wellington on one side and the grey waters of the Derwent estuary on the other. Hunt led them up a highly polished blackwood staircase to the next storey, where a few older men were sitting round in deep armchairs reading newspapers. One old codger slumbered in a corner, snorting occasionally. An antique grandfather clock ticked steadily adding to the soporific atmosphere. It was a timeless scene of discreet upper-class privilege. 'This is the members' lounge,' Hunt informed them pompously. 'We always have a few here in the mornings, but we tend to fill up later in the day.'

Ten minutes later, Jack and Liz were standing outside on the footpath, turning up their collars against the wind.

'Well,' Liz ruminated. 'Now I've seen how our betters live!'

Jack shook his head. '"A man's a man for a' that", Liz, but what did you think of Hunt?'

'You've been listening to Simon Calvert, our Red pathologist,' Liz teased. Jack said nothing. 'Well, I was watching Hunt pretty closely.' She fished out her car keys and gestured that they should get in out of the cold. 'He didn't give anything away, but I dunno ...' She unlocked the car and they both climbed in. She switched on the ignition, put the heater up to maximum and pushed in a Van Morrison tape that she knew Jack liked: 'Days Like This'.

Jack knew what she meant. 'Yeah,' he said, clicking his seatbelt closed. 'I dunno either. There was something fishy about the bugger.'

'The place, too,' Liz went on. 'I'm trying to work out what it was.' She turned on the indicator and swung the car out into the traffic, both of them listening to the music. Back in the club, Morrison Hunt had already riffled through his Filofax and was reaching for the telephone, with a look of cold fury on his corpulent features.

Jack's telephone was ringing insistently when they got back to the cop shop. Commander Holmes was on the line. 'Yes, sir,' said Jack. 'We'll be there in a couple of minutes.' He turned to Liz, who was taking off her coat. 'The boss wants to see us,' he shrugged. 'Not hard to guess what it's about.'

Liz pushed her arms back into the sleeves of her coat and they set off to Holmes's office. Holmes didn't waste time with preliminaries and didn't offer tea. 'Jack, Liz,' he intoned, running a hand through the white stripe in his hair. 'You've been upsetting some people.'

Liz looked angelic and Jack pretended he didn't know what the boss was getting at 'Upsetting people? Who do you mean, sir?'

Holmes raised an eyebrow and tapped the side of his nose. 'You know exactly who I mean, Jack. I've just had a call from a Mr Morrison Hunt. He claims you two barged into the Van Diemen Club and started making wild allegations.' He sat and waited for a reply.

Liz spoke, keeping her voice calm. 'Sir, that isn't the way it happened. I can assure you that we were on our professional best behaviour.'

'Oh, I believe you, Sergeant Flakemore, but why were you there?'

'Well, sir, I took two of the Taroona girls for a tour of the city. I was hoping that they might be able to identify the premises they were taken to.'

'And they did?' asked the Commander.

'Yes, sir. Both girls recognised the Van Diemen Club premises.'

'Hmm, you do realise who we're dealing with here?' Holmes was absently pushing his fountain pen around on his blotter.

Jack leaned forward and spoke a little more firmly than usual. 'Yes, sir. Criminals who have trafficked children.' He had steel in his voice.

Holmes sighed theatrically and shook his head slowly, looking at both in turn. 'OK, Jack, Liz. I hope that you have the evidence because these people are very well-connected. They can make things very difficult for us.'

Jack and Liz relaxed in their chairs and exchanged a glance. He'd said, 'for us', not 'for you'.

'Yes sir,' Liz agreed. 'Look, I know that we only have the girls' word for it at this stage, but there is definitely something not right about that place. Now that Morrison Hunt has got straight on the blower, I feel even more strongly that something's going on.'

'Well, you know these people feel entitled,' said Holmes. 'They'd complain even if they've done nothing. Now, the question is, what can we do about them? If we go charging in and upset them again, they will use their connections to make things very, very difficult for us.'

Jack was looking pensive.

'Yes, Jack. You *have* been listening, I hope.'

'Sorry sir. It just struck me that there's something odd about the building itself. It was when that Hunt fellow took us upstairs.' Liz was nodding, understanding dawning on her face, and Jack continued. 'It was if there was a floor *missing*.'

'A floor missing?' Holmes queried, raising an eyebrow. 'How so?'

Liz took over. 'Yes! Well, there was too big a gap between the ground and first floor. As if there was another floor tucked in between.'

'OK,' said Holmes. 'I want you to see if you can check this out. Do not go back upsetting Hunt—he's a vindictive prick with friends in high places—but see what you can find.'

***

That evening, Jack and Liz parked in Macquarie Street on the other side of the block and walked around until they could see the back of the Van Diemen Club. Liz had brought her binoculars and she trained them on the building from a vantage point in a small clump of trees next to a doctor's surgery. 'Aha!' she said. 'There are what look like bricked-up small windows above the ceiling level of the ground floor rooms.'

Jack took the glasses and took a long look. 'Yep,' he said, handing back the binoculars. 'There's definitely some low-ceilinged rooms hidden in the building.'

'Could be an innocent explanation, I suppose,' Liz replied.

'Could be, but I don't believe it,' said Jack. 'We are going to have to convince the boss to issue a warrant to do a proper search of the place. In the meantime, we can't do anything to alert our Mr Hunt and his mates.' His teeth had begun to chatter. 'Now, I could murder a curry and Wendy's promised one, so why don't you come up to Darcy Street?'

Liz readily agreed.

CHAPTER 38

JACK WAS APPLYING FOR A SEARCH WARRANT for the Van Diemen Club when Senior Sergeant Peter Bronson's balding head poked round his door. 'Got a minute, sir?' he asked, chewing on a match. The man was a two-pack-a-day smoker and needed to have something in his mouth. Jack waved him in, and Bronson got straight to the point. 'We've just pulled in a bloke for kiddie porn on his computer. Disgusting stuff. Anyway, he's trying to bargain with us. Says he has important information about a case of yours.'

'I'm all ears,' Jack replied, sitting up straight.

'Well, come down to the interview room and hear what he has to say.'

The bloke was sitting in the interview room playing with an empty cigarette packet. His brief, a trim little gent called Andrew Barnaby, was writing something in a leather-bound notebook. He looked up over halfmoon spectacles and nodded affably to Jack. A bored looking uniform was leaning again the wall, ignoring them.

'OK, thanks Dave,' said Bronson. 'Me and Jack will take it from here.'

Dave left the room and Bronson switched on the recording equipment and explained that Inspector Jack Martin had joined the interview with Jake Nelson. Nelson was a burly, sandy-haired man with guileless blue eyes and an open boyish face. When you got closer, you could see grey streaks in his hair and a network of lines belying the boyishness. When he spoke, it was with an American twang and he sounded as wholesome as mom and apple pie. He actually used the phrase 'aw shucks.' Jack knew that first impressions can deceive. Bronson had arrested Nelson as part of an operation against a kiddie porn ring. They had raided his Sandy Bay flat and seized his computer, which contained a vast trove of images. They were, said Bronson, among the most disturbing things he had ever seen in all his years of policing. He had grilled Nelson for many hours, but the man stuck obstinately to his story that someone else must have hacked into his computer and put the images there. He had never seen them. Information received from the Houston, Texas, police department, however, established that Nelson had served time in a federal penitentiary for similar crimes. When Bronson confronted with him with this, Andrew Barnaby asked to confer with his client in private. After they had consulted, Barnaby announced that his client wanted to make a deal. If they would go easy on him, he could provide information on a more serious racket. The two detectives referred the matter to Commander Holmes. If Nelson told them what he knew, they would put in a word for a lesser sentence. If he held anything back, they would throw the book at him.

When they returned, Nelson had his chubby legs sprawled

out under the table and greeted the two detectives with a grin and a 'howdy'. A Texas drawl it seemed. The fellow appeared to have no shame. Jack wondered if he had any idea of what life was like over in the Pink Palace, where the prisoners made child sex offenders' lives such a misery that they had to live in a special section. Along with Gordon Paisley, the ex-detective.

Barnaby closed his notebook and cleared his throat to speak. 'It's probably best if you hear what my client has to say,' he offered. 'I assure you that you will find it very valuable.'

Jack nodded his agreement and Nelson began to tell his story.

'Well, folks,' he said, settling in as if for a pleasant after-dinner chat. 'I work as a pilot. It's all off the books as you might say, for reasons that y'all will understand when I explain. Anyway, I'm in this country illegal for a start. I fly light aircraft and helicopters for Stephen Abercrombie and Alan Bull. I learned to fly in Vietnam. I been working for them a couple years now since I came to Australia. They was instrumental in getting me into the country and with my record I was mighty grateful to them for it. Mighty grateful, indeed, but I soon realised that they wasn't about to let me go straight.

'You see, I don't rightly like being the way I am. There's some that says there's nothing durn wrong with it, but that's not the way I think. I was raised hardshell Baptist and I knows my scripture. What's right is right and what's wrong is wrong, as my daddy always told me.'

Jack willed him to get on with it.

'I want y'all to know that although I had them pitchers on my computer, I never touched no kids—'

Bronson couldn't help it. 'Yes, but someone else hurt those kids when they were filming them. You can't absolve yourself of blame like that.'

'Now, now Sergeant Bronson,' Barnaby chided. 'Best to let Mr Nelson continue without interruption.'

Bronson raised his hands in surrender and Nelson continued.

'Anyways, I'll get back to my story,' said Nelson with a wink. 'At first, the job was straight up. I flew Mr Bull about, mainly, on business trips and to his place up on the New South Wales coast. They paid durn good money and I wasn't complaining. Occasionally, too, I'd fly Stephen Abercrombie someplace and mebbe his wife too.' He took a sip of coffee and went on.

'Mebbes 'bout a year back, Mr Abercrombie called and said he had a "special assignment" for me. Them were his words—special assignment—and them's the words he and Mr Bull always used after that. Never called a spade a spade. Turns out, I was to pick up some packages and deliver 'em to Tasmania. That become a regular thing. Sometimes to Tassie, sometimes to other places. I was based at a private airstrip near Gisborne, outside of Melbourne. They never told me what they was, but I knew they'd be drugs. I said nothing. Wasn't my place and like I say, they was paying top dollar.

'Now, you might say that by this time I was complicit in what they was doing. I thought about it but figured I was lucky to have the job, with my background, so I kept my mouth shut. Next thing was there was three kids. A Russkie by the name o' Sergey brought them. I never knew his other name. Anyways, Sergey loaded 'em into the aircraft and got in hisself.

'They was drugged up and didn't cause me no problems. They didn't tell me where they come from and I didn't ask, but I figured they was from Southeast Asia someplace, me being a Vietnam vet.'

Jack interrupted him there. 'You say these kids were brought from Asia? Do you know how they got here and who brought them?'

'Well, Inspector, I didn't ask a helluva lot of questions, but I did hear Mr Bull or Mr Abercrombie say that we was at the end of a big chain organised by a Russian outfit. They sometimes flew over oceans. Sometimes they brought what they called the merchandise in big fishing boats or even freighters. As I say, I didn't want to know too much, If I knew something more than that, I'd tell you.'

'So Stephen Abercombie or Alan Bull would know?' asked Jack. 'What about the man who called himself Kuznetsov? Or another man called Smirnov?'

'Reckon they would, Mr Martin, but I guess you'd be better off asking them.'

Jack nodded and Nelson continued. 'Since then, I done a couple similar runs. Mebbe three or four. I'd pick 'em up near Gisborne an' fly 'em over to an airstrip near Huonville. What happened to 'em afterwards I couldn't say because Sergey drove 'em off straightaway. I figured it was bad, but then it wasn't my business to ask.'

A penny dropped inside Jack's head. Christ! There had been an aircraft circling around the Huon when he was up there a while back hiking with Liz. If only he had investigated!

'Anyways, Alan Bull has a property set in the hills at the back of White Beach on the Tasman Peninsula. It's between there and Port Arthur. Big white house set up on a hill with a horse stud there. I never stayed there. Never went in. Just dropped off the live—the kids, and lit out. It was the same pack drill as before. I'd fly Mr Bull down and he'd ring me after a week, mebbe, and I'd take the helicopter down there and pick him up, take him to the airstrip and then fly him back to Victoria.'

'Helicopter?' asked Jack, his ears pricked. 'You said there was a helicopter.'

'Yeah, that's what I said. Bell Jetranger. Nice. Anyways, one day a feller they call Sokolov was at the Tassie airstrip with that other Russkie, Sergey. They had one of the kids with them, all drugged up. I flew the chopper down to the place near White Beach and Alan Bull come and got the kid. Told me he'd ring to say when to come back. It happened maybe four or five times. Sometimes a boy. Sometimes a girl. Always drugged up so that they was docile, Mr Martin. Now, if I might trouble you for another cup of coffee, I'd be grateful because I have a big difficulty talking about what comes next.'

Bronson went to the door and ordered a passing constable

to bring more coffee and some biscuits. While they were waiting, Jack asked about Vietnam. Nelson said he had done two tours of service there, piloting helicopter gunships. It was there, Nelson said, that he had 'developed his tastes' in the fleshpots of Saigon. The coffee arrived; Nelson drank it greedily and signalled that he was ready to continue. Bronson restarted the tape.

'Couple weeks ago,' Nelson continued. 'I took a boy down there to Bull's property, well-drugged-up as usual by Sokolov and Sergey. I come back a couple days later when Bull rang and picked the boy up. Bull had given him something to quiet him, but he was sobbing, and I felt kinda sorry for him to tell you the truth. It hit me then what it would be like to be in his shoes. I'd never really given it much thought about where they'd got these kids from, but I had a good idea of what they did with them. Sokolov told me there was some fancy club where they took 'em in Hobart. He was laughing about it. A cold fish was Sokolov. Russkie with a big scar on his face and steel teeth. Yeah, steel teeth, man!

'Anyways, to get back to the story, I was flying back to the Huonville strip over the bush towards the coast. On the Tasman Peninsula, I mean. I remember looking down and seeing a guy ploughing his field with a horse, just like my grandpappy did. The kid wasn't as drugged up as I thought. He managed to open the side door of the chopper and before I could stop him, he had jumped out. Weren't a durned thing I could do about it.' He paused and slurped his coffee.

'I banked the chopper to see but he had fallen from quite a height. We was almost over the cliffs north of Cape Raoul—I liked to fly about there for the view—and I could see a little patch of orange on the clifftop. Just a bit farther and he would have fallen into the sea. Mebbe the big sailing boat that was passing would have picked him up if he had, but he woulda been just as dead, I figured. There was nothing I could do but head for home.' He spread his hands to indicate that he was finished.

Jack stood up and muttered to Bronson that he had to go. There was no way he could remain in the same room to breathe the same air as Nelson. Had he not been arrested for the pornographic images on his computer there was no reason to believe that he would not have continued to ferry the kids around. He hadn't developed a conscience. Nelson would have a few years taken off his sentence and would get out to re-offend back in the States when he'd been deported. Jack wasn't even sure whether they wouldn't have tracked Bull down to his lair because he had already worked out that the man would be holed up somewhere down near Port Arthur. They would go and find him. Whatever he thought of Nelson, they now knew how the boy—Icarus—had got to be on Shipstern Bluff that hot summer's day. And they had some inkling of the extent and size of the trafficking operation.

CHAPTER 39

LATE THAT SAME MORNING, Jack walked up the front steps of the Van Diemen Club. Liz and Duncan Snodgers were standing behind him, together with the two young officers, Kate Farrar and Barney Hurst, in plain clothes again. Uniformed officers were standing on the footpath and Bluey Bishop was round the back. 'Come on,' Jack muttered impatiently. 'Open the bloody door.' A fine drizzle was leaking from the sky and cars were swishing past on the wet road. Jack felt a pleasant sense of anticipation. On the other hand, if he were wrong, there would be some major repercussions.

'You again,' sniffed Morrison Hunt. 'I made it clear that you were barking up the wrong tree.'

Jack waved the warrant at him and the team barged past. 'Now, go to your office and stay there,' he ordered. 'Nobody is to leave the premises. Kate, escort Mr Hunt to his office and make sure he doesn't use the telephone. I'll collect him shortly.'

Jack and Liz went straight to the blackwood staircase and began to inspect the walls, with Duncan following along behind, wheezing at the exertion. They stopped at the landing and ran their hands around the walls. The join was faint, but once you'd seen it, you couldn't miss it. There was a door set into the panelling. Jack pushed but it didn't move. He removed the John Glover painting—it really did look like an original up close—and there, under where it had been, was a keyhole.

'Liz, get Hunt up here, please,' he ordered. 'With his keys.'

Hunt appeared at the foot of the stairs, trying to look indignant. Jack crooked a finger and summoned him to the landing. 'What's this, Mr Hunt?' he demanded, pointing at the keyhole.

'Oh that,' Hunt replied. 'It's just a storeroom, I think.'

'Really?' said Jack, raising an eyebrow. 'Open it.'

'I, err, don't know if I have the key.' Sweat began to gleam on Hunt's forehead.

'Mr Hunt, I find it impossible to believe that you don't. You're the club secretary, for Christ's sake. Now open it or we will break it down!

While Hunt was fumbling with his keys, Jack asked why the door was so well hidden. Hunt opened his mouth, closed it, and then left it open. When the door swung open, fluorescent lights flickered on automatically inside, revealing a low corridor with four doors along one side. Hunt was looking pale, and all trace of his suave arrogance was gone.

'What is this place?' Jack demanded.

Hunt shrugged. 'Err, it's for when the country members have had a bit too much to drink and can't drive home.'

His eyes slid sideways, and he began perspiring again when Jack pushed the first door open. The little room contained a bed, a small dressing table, and a sink. There was a tall mirror on the wall. The other rooms had identical furnishings, except for one that had mirrors on the ceiling.

Duncan called Jack back. 'Och,' he said. 'I want everybody to keep oot, no exceptions.'

Jack called down the staircase to Barney and Kate. 'Handcuffs please,' he said. 'Take this gentleman to the station and arrange some lodgings for him.'

Hunt slunk off between the two officers, his shoulders slumped, and his head bowed. When Jack got back to the station, however, he found the man had recovered a little. After conferring with his solicitor—Andrew Barnaby again—he agreed to answer questions.

'It's for the sake of the club,' he insisted. 'Most of the members know nothing about ... about what was happening. I knew, of course, and I'm prepared to face the consequences, but I cannot tell you who was involved in the, err, incidents.'

'Cannot or will not?' Jack demanded.

Hunt said nothing. He was formally charged with trafficking children, unlawful detention, and aiding and abetting the rape of minors, and led off to the cells. Like Jake Nelson, he would be up before the magistrate in the morning. Jack hoped that Duncan Snodgers would get enough evidence to find Hunt's associates. They would have another go at Hunt the following day after he'd spent the night in the cells with a wino and a steel toilet for company.

CHAPTER 40

THE NEXT MORNING DAWNED COLD AND CLEAR. Jack and Bluey left the police station early, heading for the Tasman Peninsula. Constable Pru Skinner was waiting in her police car by the creek at White Beach. Bluey parked behind her car and they joined her.

'Should I turn the siren on, sir?' she asked as she started the engine.

'Nah, I don't think so,' Jack replied. 'He's slippery, so let's not let him know we're coming.'

Skinner turned into a narrow dirt road near the beach and drove inland through scrubby forest until they reached some rolling grassland. Skinner filled them in with what she knew about Bull. The locals knew him as Toby Wolf, she said; a bull-necked fat man who kept to himself and was rarely seen except when he was on his way to or from the big white yacht he kept tethered in Barilla Bay. They had heard the helicopter coming and going, but thought it was a rich man's toy and forgot about it.

They came to a big gate with a sign announcing TAURUS STUD TRESPASSERS PROSECUTED. There were some beautiful horses grazing in the paddocks and a few sheep were nibbling the grass near the roadside. They looked up nervously when Jack jumped out and pushed the gate open. It was still quite a way to the house, which sat on a wooded ridge with tremendous views down towards the coast. There was a vineyard on a north-facing slope and a cluster of stables and other buildings. The stone house itself was handsome, with a wide veranda and a row of dormer windows set into the steeply pitched roof. It reeked of money and a butler emerged and asked their business.

'Police,' said Jack. 'We're here to see Alan Bull.' He produced his warrant card and held it up for the man to see.

'Very well sir,' said the butler. 'I'll check to see if Mr Bull is available.'

'He'd better be,' Bluey muttered. 'This isn't a social call.'

The butler came back out and said that Mr Bull would see them in the drawing room. Drawing room, thought Jack, what kind of transplanted Pommy nonsense was this? They found Bull waiting for them with his elbow on the mantlepiece, drinking a glass of what looked like sherry. He put the glass down and turned to greet them. He was short and fat, and dressed in a light grey suit, with highly polished brogues on his little feet. He had no neck. His head was almost bald, but he had combed a few strands of blond-grey hair over his pate. He surveyed them with sharp grey eyes and had a disdainful sneer on his face.

'Yes,' he invited, as if he was doing them a favour. 'What can I do for you?' He looked at his watch—an expensive Cartier thing—as if he were only prepared to give them a small amount of his precious time.

'Alan Bull?' Jack queried.

'Yes, I am,' the fat man agreed.

'In that case, I am arresting you for human trafficking, false imprisonment, rape and sexual abuse of minors. You do not have to say anything, but anything you do say may be used in evidence.'

Bull paled and stiffened but managed to replace his disdain with an attempt at outrage. He huffed and puffed about seeing his lawyer, but Jack nodded to Constable Skinner and she moved forward quickly and clicked handcuffs around his wrists. It gave Jack huge satisfaction to push the man's head down as they bundled him into the police car. Bull made noises about the people he knew, but Jack told him to shut up and Bluey gave him such a look that he subsided into silence.

Late that afternoon, with Bull safely banged up in the cells, the murder team retired to the pub to celebrate. The gang was effectively broken, with only Sokolov/Smirnov and the man known as Sergey unaccounted for. Popov was locked up in Melbourne and Abercrombie would soon be in custody in Hobart. Melbourne police were also rounding up Popov's operatives in that city and had sent important information to NSW about the activities of another offshoot of the gang in Sydney and the Central Coast. All of this amounted to a significant victory, but the Van Diemen Club still needed cleaning out. Unfortunately, while there were many fingerprints in the secret rooms, none were a match for anyone on file. It seemed that Hunt was a provider rather than a user and that Bull had never visited the club, preferring to have his loathsome fun in private.

Jack made his apologies early at the pub where the team were celebrating. Normally, he would have stayed on, but he had to get to his Italian lesson. Francesca was already there, and she smiled a welcome. Jack almost believed that there might be a god after all. They agreed that they would meet the following week for coffee and Jack didn't cringe when Ms Locatelli berated him for not doing his homework.

CHAPTER 41

THE NEXT MORNING'S BRIEFING was short and to the point. Many of the traffickers were behind bars, Jack announced, but there were still some more running around free. One of them was a Russian gangster called Smirnov. The other was his accomplice Sergey Petrov. Their mugshots had been circulated but they had gone to ground. Petrov was the gang's driver and because of this he would have important information that would enable them to completely clean up the trafficking operation. 'Let's find them,' said Jack, winding up the briefing. The detectives scurried off. Jack couldn't help smirking. Many of them had obvious hangovers, and while they were boozing, he had spent a blameless evening learning Italian and getting to know Francesca. Liz noticed his grin. 'Holier than thou, eh?' she said with a wink.

Jack was walking back to his office when Chris Chambers, the desk sergeant, waved to get his attention. 'Oh Jack,' said Chambers, 'there's a young woman in the waiting room to see you. She said that she'd only speak to you.'

Jack recognised the young blonde woman as Samantha Towns, one of the girls he'd spoken with at Trixie Ashford's house. She was dressed this time in runners, toucan jumper, and jeans, with a New Norfolk footy scarf and beanie because of the cold. She was biting her fingernails nervously and stood up quickly when she saw him. Jack greeted her civilly and she smiled shyly.

'Some of the other girls would kill me for coming here,' she said, 'but I don't care anymore. Trixie's been shut down and I'm thinking about going interstate. What I want to tell you about is them blokes and the kids.'

'You'd better come through,' Jack replied. 'I'll get you a cup of tea or coffee and you can sit where it's a bit warmer. I'll get Sergeant Flakemore to join us if you don't mind.'

Samantha sipped her tea gratefully and Jack waited for her to begin. Liz was sitting unobtrusively at the rear of the office. Samantha sat the mug down carefully on the edge of the desk and started her story.

'There was this guy who come into the err ... brothel a few times. A foreign bloke. He was my client a coupla times, you know. Anyway, I sorta liked him.' She took another sip of tea and Jack rummaged around in his desk and showed her the identikit picture of Ivan Smirnov. 'No, it wasn't him, Mr Martin, although I seen him around the place a lot. The bloke I mean was younger.'

'Was it this one?' Jack asked, proffering the identikit drawing of the gang's driver, Sergey Petrov.

Samantha took the picture and studied it carefully. 'Yeah, that's him. His face is sorta thinner, but I recognise him.'

'Sergey Petrov?'

'Yeah. I never knew his surname, but that's him. Anyway,

as I said, I sorta liked him and when he asked for a how can I put it, home visit, I agreed.'

Jack and Liz exchanged glances.

'Anyway, he lived in a big house up on Poets Road. You know, the street that runs off Landsdowne Crescent in West Hobart.' Jack nodded. 'Like I was saying. I liked him. You don't ask no questions in this game, but he told me he was Russian, and he was saving up so that he could go home and start up a business. I never asked him what he done here.'

'Do you know the number of the Poets Road place?' asked Jack, sitting up attentively.

'Yeah, no worries. I wrote it down in case I forgot. Got it here.' She rummaged in her pocket and handed Jack the note.

'So, if I may, Samantha,' asked Jack. 'Why did you decide to tell us about this now?'

'Well, I was havin' coffee with Jenny—she's one of the other girls from Trixie's—and she started teasing me about Sergey. Reckoned I had the hots for him. I was sorta playing along with it, you know, but then she told me that Sergey was mixed up with that lot in the factory. The ones who were pimping out the kids and that.' Samantha started biting her nails again. 'That's all I know, Mr Martin.'

'Samantha,' Jack replied. 'You've done the right thing. Now, would you like another cup of tea or anything?'

'I'm right with this, thank you,' Samantha replied. There was obviously something else on her mind. 'I never liked being on the game, Mr Martin. I just sorta drifted into it because I was never no good at school. Left early and got a few shitty jobs and so … well, the money was better. But you see, Mr Martin, I'd like to get away from it now. I dunno if you could put me in touch with anyone that could help?'

Liz spoke now. She knew some people who could help and arranged to put Samantha in touch with them: a feminist group that included some women who had been on the game. 'They're not god-botherers, Samantha. They won't judge you and they can help.'

Jack escorted Samantha to the front door and thanked her again for her help. He watched her as she walked off down the street. He didn't judge her either, but someone who did was standing there.

'Seeing off your little prozzy friend,' sneered Eric Blundstone. 'Any chance of a freebie?'

Jack rounded on him furiously. 'Thanking a member of the public for important information,' Jack hissed, getting right in the man's face. 'And it's sir to you, *Senior Constable Blundstone*. Now if you haven't any work to do, I'll arrange some for you.'

Blundstone slunk off, his body language tense and angry.

CHAPTER 42

THE BIG RED BRICK HOUSE was nestled high up under the slopes of Knocklofty in West Hobart, with tremendous views over the city and out over the sea to Cape Raoul. Jack had briefed the crew that the man they were seeking was dangerous and probably armed. The officers were wearing bulletproof vests and the response unit wore helmets and carried automatic rifles. The house sat in overgrown grounds and a big dark blue van was sitting in the driveway, which rose steeply from the road. Jack directed some of the officers into the cul-de-sac at the back of the house and sent in the armed unit. They smashed in the front door with the enforcer and piled inside going from room to room checking for the suspect. Petrov rushed out of the back door and was sprinting across the back lawn when Kate Farrar brought him down with a flying tackle. 'Gotcha!' she cried as Barney Hurst rushed up and clicked handcuffs around Petrov's wrists. Farrar took the Makarov pistol from Petrov's waistband. Petrov said nothing, which might have been because his face was pushed into the grass. 'You are nicked, Mr Petrov!' said Kate delightedly, dragging him to his feet and shoving him back into the house.

Petrov was a tall, gaunt young man with cropped brown hair and a narrow face with slanting Slavic cheekbones. There were deep, unhealed scratch marks down one side of his face. He didn't look at all happy when they put him in a cell and a little while later when they took him through to an interview room he looked as if he was about to cry. He opened his mouth to say something when Jack walked in with Constable Farrar and turned on the recording apparatus. Jack raised a finger, cautioning him to remain quiet while he fiddled with the equipment. When he had it working properly, he introduced himself and Kate Farrar and read Petrov his rights. Petrov shook his head when Jack asked if he wanted a lawyer.

'Now, Mr Petrov,' said Jack. 'This is just a preliminary interview. You are entitled to legal representation, so if you like, I can arrange for the duty solicitor to come.'

Petrov's English was shaky. He hadn't really needed to speak it for most of the time since he entered the country, but he knew enough to be able to follow the questions— just—so Jack halted the proceedings and brought in Irina Chernyshevsky to translate. Constable Chernyshevsky was a forty-something woman who worked in Traffic and spoke excellent English with a hint of a Russian accent. Petrov looked almost relieved when the big woman addressed him in Russian.

'Now,' said Jack. 'You wanted to say something when we first came into the room.' He waited for Irina to translate and waited for Petrov's response, which came in a gush of Russian.

'He says,' said Irina, 'that he wants to make a full confession, but if he does, he wants immunity from prosecution.'

'So, he wants to turn Queen's evidence?'

'Yes, that is what he is saying, Jack.'

Petrov was speaking again in rapid Russian and Irina translated again. 'He is saying that he knows everything about the gang. He was the driver for Mr Kuznetsov in Melbourne and for the gang in Hobart. He says that if he gives evidence, he wants immunity. You can deport him to Russia.'

'OK,' Jack replied. 'Tell him that we must clear this with Commander Holmes. If he agrees, we'll proceed, but I must warn him that he must tell us absolutely everything. If he holds anything back or tells any lies, any deal that we make will be null and void.'

Petrov nodded when Irina translated. Jack made him agree verbally and suspended the interview. Petrov was escorted back to the cells and Jack took Constable Farrar with him to see Commander Holmes. He had been very impressed with Farrar's work and that of Constable Hurst and was thinking of recommending their transfer to the CIB. Meanwhile, Duncan Snodgers and his overworked crew were crawling all over the dark blue van taken from the house in Poets Road.

Derek Holmes waved Jack and Kate to seats and Jack explained the situation. 'Although we are pretty sure that we've broken the back of the trafficking gang, we still need evidence on their customers. The Van Diemen Club secretary is refusing to give us any names and we can expect that "people with influence"—he made air quotes—will try to frustrate the investigation at every twist and turn. Petrov has been intimately involved with the gang, but I think it's a good trade-off if he fingers some of the Club culprits for us.'

'And we'll deport him once the trials are over?' Holmes was looking thoughtfully out the window overlooking Liverpool Street. 'OK, let's do it, but as you say, any funny business and the deal is off. I'll have to ok it with the higher-ups, of course.'

Once they returned to the interview room, Petrov began to sing like the proverbial canary. He had, he confessed, driven almost all the consignments of kids and drugs to and from the Huonville airstrip and around the city. He had also overseen a network of dealers who sold 'product' on the streets. Custard Sproule, Les Jetson, and Sean Hurd had reported to him in this matter. He had forced the old Mitropoulos firm off the streets, threatening them with the Makarov. He confirmed that Jake Nelson had flown individual victims down to Alan Bull and named Ivan Sokolov (Smirnov), Stephen Abercrombie, Popov, and Trixie Ashford as other leaders of the crime syndicate. He also sketched in the international channels along which product and human beings were smuggled. Those kidnapped in the Balkans and Southeast Asia included children of both sexes and adult women, who were put to work in the syndicate's mainland brothels. Petrov also put his hand up to delivering kids to the Van Diemen Club and returning them to the Taroona and Glenorchy houses afterwards. Petrov always helped take the children from his van into the club premises and would spend the evenings drinking in the club bar. These excursions were always made late at night while the bulk of the club's members were absent. Morrison Hunt was a facilitator who, to his knowledge, never touched the children. He named eight club members who regularly paid to abuse the kids, all of them prominent citizens, well-connected politically and socially. He'd learned this to provide himself with insurance. Asked if there were any others who abused the children, Petrov said he did not know, although it was possible. He had never entered the secret rooms himself, but the men he named would congregate in the bar and ply him with drinks. Jack was already planning a line-up to identify the miscreants.

'Did it occur to you that what was happening was wrong, and that you were part of this wrongdoing?' Jack asked him through the interpreter. Petrov shrugged his narrow shoulders. He was an orphan who had been recruited back in Moscow and had steadily fallen deeper and deeper into the gang's activities. By the time he arrived in Australia along the same illegal channels as the kids and drugs, it was too late for him to get out. People such as Smirnov, Kuznetzov and Bull were terrifying individuals and he feared that they would not hesitate to kill him if he did not obey orders.

'And where will you go if we deport you?' Jack asked.

'I will change name and disappear. Siberia, I think,' Petrov replied. 'I cannot live in Moscow because gang would kill me.'

When he had switched off the recording equipment, Jack asked Petrov what had happened to his face. It had been disturbing him throughout the session. The wounds only just stopped short of his eye and they looked infected.

Petrov pulled a face. 'Wildcat,' he muttered.

Jack hoped that one of the kids had done it to him. The Cambodian kid, Nornry, she was a feisty little thing to have escaped from the gang. He'd lay odds it was her.

'Cambodian wildcat, I think,' he told Petrov and the man shrugged. 'Doctor says she probably has HIV/AIDS.' Petrov blanched and Jack laughed all the way back to his office. The kid had nothing of the sort, but he'd put the fear of death into the gangster turned informer. He couldn't get off completely scot-free.

It no longer mattered that Morrison Hunt was refusing to cooperate with the investigation. Duncan Snodgers had been beavering away and had accumulated a mountain of forensic evidence from the secret rooms, including hair, dried semen, and fingerprints. The blue van had been dismantled and the fingerprints inside matched with those of the trafficked children, including the nameless boy who had died on Shipstern Bluff. A white van had been found nearby. Jack had also seized the Van Diemen Club membership records and guest book. They would fingerprint the entire membership if necessary and compare their prints with those found in the secret rooms. The suspects—and this meant the entire membership as far as Jack was concerned—told all kinds of lies and resorted to legal shenanigans to obstruct the investigation, but in the end, they were required to submit to fingerprinting and saliva swabbing. A couple more members were found to have availed themselves of the children, which brought the total number of confirmed abusers to ten, all of them from Hobart's great and good.

The ten suspects were arrested, some at their homes and others in their places of employment, all of them protesting their innocence and vowing retribution. Bail was denied and they found themselves in the remand section of Risdon Prison until threats from other prisoners caused them to be placed in special confinement. Two of them managed to commit suicide while on remand—one by hanging himself and the other from an overdose of drugs smuggled in from outside. The trials were a sensation, both locally and nationally and were even reported in the *New York Times* and other leading world newspapers. Sergey Petrov made a compelling witness and despite their denials, three solicitors were found guilty and sentenced to long terms of imprisonment. They were joined by Morrison Hunt, a pair of accountants and a rich idler who had been seeking pre-selection as a parliamentary candidate in the conservative interest. Two others were acquitted for lack of firm evidence. Custard Sproule, Sean Hurd and Jake Nelson joined the silvertail crims in the Pink Palace. Trixie Ashford, Alan Bull and Stephen Abercrombie were also put away for lengthy terms. They would all serve long sentences among other sex offenders in separate confinement away from the general prison population, who hated 'kiddie fiddlers' with a passion. The Van Diemen Club closed its doors before the trials and the property was put up for sale. Also languishing behind bars was William 'Billy' Bloat. It had come out at his trial that he had been disarmed by the 86-year-old Beryl Ross and he was a laughingstock as a result—a real comedown for the ferocious Mad Dog of the Ulster Freedom Fighters.

Mr Sokolov, aka Ivan Smirnov, had vanished.

EPILOGUE

TWO YEARS LATER, workers demolishing the old Jones Firebird steel fabrication shop made a grisly discovery. After shifting a stack of the lighter girders in the yard with a Fowler crane, the rigger Scrooge Johnstone bent down to tie his boot-lace and shot back up, goggle-eyed. 'Jesus Christ!' he roared to the crane driver. 'It's fuckin' horrible!' 'Whatsit now?' scoffed his mate, 'Snake or something?' He also stood wide-eyed when he climbed out of his crane and saw the skeletal human hand protruding from the ground. The forefinger stuck up rudely, 'like it was givin' us the finger!' Scrooge told his wife when he got home. The men had scurried over to the site office and dialled 000. Jack guessed that the corpse was that of the elusive Mr Sokolov, whose mother had known him as Ivan Smirnov. When they had exhumed the remains, pathologist Simon Calvert drew attention to its stainless-steel false teeth, which had been common in Soviet dentistry. 'You can file 'em to keep 'em sharp,' he joked. 'Bite through anything like butter!' The Makarov pistol found beside him in the grave was a further pointer to the corpse's identity.

Calvert discounted suicide, although the only fingerprints on the weapon were Sokolov/Smirnov's. 'He's been shot in the leg and the entry angle of the bullet in the head doesn't fit. Someone else shot him and wiped their prints off the gun.'

Jack agreed. His thoughts turned to Custard Sproule, Sean Hurd, and the awful Trixie Ashford. Maybe one of them had shot this fellow. When he interviewed her at the Pink Palace, Ashford denied all knowledge of the corpse. He wouldn't put anything past the old thing, but he had no evidence that it was her. He wondered about Custard and Sean, who certainly had the motive and the opportunity. They were terrified of Smirnov. Perhaps they feared they would be his next victims? As for the means, well, it was possible that they'd overpowered Smirnov, although he doubted it. The man was a Spetsnaz veteran, a highly trained killer, and they were cheap Hobart spivs who preyed on the weak. Maybe Smirnov had tried to get one of them to execute the other, as he had done with Les Jetson, and they had turned the gun on him instead. They denied it and he could not prove otherwise. Alan Bull might have done it, but there was no evidence he'd ever visited the factory. Stephen Abercrombie most definitely had been there, but he didn't fit the bill. He was useless as an ashtray on a motor bike, a Scotch old boy out of his depth in a murderous conspiracy. Jack had to admit that part of him didn't really want to solve the murder. He knew it was his duty to find the killer, but Sokolov, or Smirnov, had deserved what he got. Jack realised that some other bastard would step into Sokolov's shoes, but at least this monster could no longer hurt people.

Returning home, Jack cast gloomy thoughts aside. The following week, he and Francesca were flying to Rome. They would first visit her relatives in Naples and then travel up to Trieste by train to see if they could find members of his family.

They had both kept up their language class, and even come to like Ms Locatelli, for her bark was worse than her bite. Now they were both reasonably proficient in the language Jack had never known and what Francesca's parents had not wanted her to learn. 'We are in a new country,' they had said. 'We are Australians now and don't need the old language.'

Jack could never forget the nameless boy who had fallen from the sky; the youngster they had called Icarus for want of better. In his mind, Jack would always hear the boy's forsaken cry. The world might have moved on, but for Jack it was an important failure not to have established his identity. Unlike the Icarus of legend, this boy had not lived long enough to make his way, and his own mistakes, in the world. His flight was not fearless, and he never felt the burning light. Jack and his colleagues had had some successes. Some vile people were locked away—although he did not kid himself that other heads of the hydra were not still alive and thriving—and the other kidnapped children had been repatriated. They had identified the child who died of neglect and repatriated her remains to her grandparents who had survived internecine war. She had a name, Besjana Dervishi. Yet to Jack's sorrow, despite extensive correspondence with the Serbian and Albanian police, they had never learned the identity of the boy who fell to Shipstern Bluff on the ocean's edge. Alan Bull couldn't or wouldn't help and had hanged himself with a bedsheet. Jack was tormented by the knowledge that back in some war-torn village in the former Yugoslavia, a family was grieving for their lost son, and would never know his fate.

Lightning Source UK Ltd.
Milton Keynes UK
UKHW010702080921
390232UK00001B/15